Edgar Wallace was born ille
adopted by George Freeman,
eleven, Wallace sold newspap
school took a job with a printer. He enlisted in the ...,
Regiment, later transferring to the Medical Staff Corps and was sent
to South Africa. In 1898 he published a collection of poems called
The Mission that Failed, left the army and became a correspondent
for Reuters.

Wallace became the South African war correspondent for *The
Daily Mail*. His articles were later published as *Unofficial Dispatches* and
his outspokenness infuriated Kitchener, who banned him as a war
correspondent until the First World War. He edited the *Rand Daily
Mail*, but gambled disastrously on the South African Stock Market,
returning to England to report on crimes and hanging trials. He
became editor of *The Evening News*, then in 1905 founded the Tallis
Press, publishing *Smith*, a collection of soldier stories, and *Four Just
Men*. At various times he worked on *The Standard*, *The Star*, *The Week-
End Racing Supplement* and *The Story Journal*.

In 1917 he became a Special Constable at Lincoln's Inn and also
a special interrogator for the War Office. His first marriage to Ivy
Caldecott, daughter of a missionary, had ended in divorce and he
married his much younger secretary, Violet King.

The Daily Mail sent Wallace to investigate atrocities in the Belgian
Congo, a trip that provided material for his *Sanders of the River* books.
In 1923 he became Chairman of the Press Club and in 1931 stood
as a Liberal candidate at Blackpool. On being offered a scriptwriting
contract at RKO, Wallace went to Hollywood. He died in 1932, on
his way to work on the screenplay for *King Kong*.

52 903 818

Bones of the River

A "Sanders of the River" book

HOUSE OF STRATUS

Copyright by Edgar Wallace

This edition published in 2001 by House of Stratus, an imprint of Stratus Holdings plc, 24c Old Burlington Street, London, W1X 1RL, UK.

www.houseofstratus.com

Typeset, printed and bound by House of Stratus.

A catalogue record for this book is available from the British Library.

ISBN 1-84232-665-1

CONTENTS

THE FEARFUL WORD

"Look after the chickens," said Hamilton sardonically, "put the cat out, and don't forget to wind up the clock."

Lieutenant Tibbetts inclined his head with, as he believed, a certain quiet dignity.

"And take something for that stiff neck of yours," added Hamilton.

Mr Commissioner Sanders came back from the deck of the *Zaire* to the little concrete quay that jutted out from the residency grounds.

He was leaving on a short tour of inspection, and with him went Captain Hamilton and half a company of Houssas. Mr Tibbetts, whose more familiar name was Bones, was staying behind in charge, and would be for seven days Deputy Commissioner, Deputy Commander of the troops, Deputy Paymaster-General, and Chief of Staff. He was also temporarily in control of twenty-five Orpington hens, three cockerels and a new fowl house, the property of his superior officer. The cat and the clock were figments of Captain Hamilton's imagination.

"And by the way" – Hamilton, one foot on the deck of the little steamer and one on the quay, turned – "cut out the fairy tales, Bones."

Mr Tibbetts raised his eyebrows patiently and looked resigned.

"If you have to entertain callers, tell 'em something useful such as: A squared plus B squared equals C squared – a little algebra would improve the moral status of the wandering Isisi."

Once before, whilst Bones had been in charge of the station, there had come a canoe from the Isisi country, carrying a small chief with a grievance to lay before the Commissioner. And Bones, being unable

1

to settle their problem, had improved the shining hour by giving them a rough-and-ready translation from Grimm. It was not a happy experiment, for when the little chief had gone back to his village he had practised the new magic, with disastrous results, for, failing to turn his nagging wife into a tree, he had, in his annoyance, beaten her so severely that she had died.

"Lord, the magic was as the lord Tibbetti told me, for I sprinkled her with water and said: 'Be thou a tree,' but because the woman has an evil mind she would not obey the lord's magic."

Bones sniffed.

"Sarcasm, my dear old commander, is wasted on me. I shall simply shut myself up with my jolly old studies and refuse to see anybody. As to your indecent old cocks and hens, I refuse absolutely to have anything to do with 'em. There's nothing in King's Regulations about looking after chickens – I hate to remind you, but you really ought to know, dear old officer, that it's not my duty to give them their milk or whatever nourishment the unfortunate animals want…"

"Good-bye, Bones," called Sanders from the bridge. "O boy, let go the big rope!"

The hawser splashed into the water, and her stern wheel moving briskly, the *Zaire* slipped to midstream and set her nose to the tawny current.

"Teach 'em the new two-step!" shouted Hamilton derisively.

"Teach your own chickens!" screeched Bones.

Lieutenant Tibbetts had three daydreams. In point of fact, he had near three hundred, but there were three favourites. The first of these had to do with the rescue of beautiful females from various dangers. Bones possessed (in his dream) a dark girl with big, luminous eyes and slim, svelte figure. And a fair girl with a complexion like milk and a figure that was not so slim; and a dashing and rather a fastish kind of girl, who got into scrapes against his earnest advice, defied him and went her own wilful way, leaving a stern young lover behind whose grief and anguish none would guess from a glance at his pale, set face. And when he rescued her, she used either to fall weeping into his arms, or fall weeping to her knees, or fall prostrate at his feet. She invariably fell one way or another, and was forgiven, or wasn't forgiven, according to the mood in which Bones happened to be.

His second dream was of digging up enormous sums of money and buying a wonderful yacht, which would be manned by silent, saturnine and mysterious men. He would sail to unknown seas and reappear unexpectedly at Cowes. It wasn't always at Cowes – but was invariably before a large, fashionable and appreciative audience. And beautiful girls would see the yacht come sailing majestically to its anchorage, and would say to one another or anybody who happened to be round:

"It is the *The Yellow Vampire* returned from one of its strange voyages. Look! That is Captain Tibbetts, the millionaire, on the bridge. They say he hates women. How I should like to know him!"

He had a third, and this was the dearest of all. It involved the discovery by the higher authorities of his extraordinary powers of organisation, his amazing knowledge of criminology, and the fear that his name inspired in the breasts of evildoers. Delicate and refined young women riding in the park would turn and gaze after his sombre figure and glance significantly at one another.

"That is Commissioner Tibbetts of the CID. Never a day passes but his ruthless hand drags a murderer to the gallows. How black and sinister his life must be! I wish I could get an introduction to him."

Bones had made many incursions into the realms of crime investigation. They had not been very successful. He had read books on criminology, and had studied learned textbooks in which scientific men with foreign names tabulated the size of criminals' ears and drew remarkable conclusions from the shapes of their noses. This branch of the study became unpopular when he found, in the shape of Captain Hamilton's eyebrow, proof positive of homicidal tendencies.

Bones lay stretched in the shade of a little matted verandah before his hut. It was a roasting hot day, with not so much as a breeze from the sea to temper the furnace-like atmosphere of headquarters.

Bones was not asleep. It was equally true that he was not awake. He was arresting a man whose crimes had baffled the police of the world until, misguidedly, he came into the orbit of that lynx-eyed sleuth, "Trailer" Tibbetts of Scotland Yard.

Suddenly the patter of bare feet, and Bones blinked and was awake. It was a lanky, barefooted corporal of Houssas, and he brought his hand stiffly to his scarlet tarbosh.

"There is a canoe from the upper country. I have told the men that they must wait until you have spoken."

"Eh?" said Bones huskily. "What's this nonsense? Arrest the man and bring him before me!"

He might have been reciting the *Iliad* for all the corporal understood, for he was speaking in English.

"Bring them," he said at last. "And, Mahmet, have you given food to the cluck-cluck?"

"Lord, you said that you yourself would carry food to the cluck-cluck. Water I gave them because they made fearful noises."

Bones screwed in his eyeglass and glared.

"Bring the men: then take food to the birds which are as the apple of Militini's eye, being his own aunts turned by enchantment – " He stopped, remembering Hamilton's warning. Bones loved fairy stories.

So there came to him M'gula of the Upper Ochori, an old man of forty, with a big head and a wrinkled face.

"I see you, Tibbetti," he boomed, as he squatted in the hot sunlight.

"I see you, man," said Bones. "Now, tell me why you have come in your big canoe. Sandi is not with me, having gone to the Isisi country, but I sit in his place and give justice." This Bones magnificently.

"Lord, I have heard of you and your wise words. From the river-with-one-bank to the mountains of the old king, people speak of you clapping their hands. It is said that you are greater than Sandi, being a magician. For you take things in your hand and they disappear. Also from the air you take silver dollars. Also it is said that from an empty pot you have drawn beautiful things, such as birds and pieces of cloth and small animals."

Bones coughed a little self-consciously. He had once performed a few conjuring tricks before an awestricken audience. Happily Hamilton knew nothing of this.

"So, lord, I came, knowing that the lord Sandi was going to the Isisi, because I have many thoughts that trouble my mind."

In a country where men have been known to travel a thousand miles to seek the answer to a riddle, it was not remarkable that one should make the long journey from the Ochori to find relief even from a trivial worry, and Bones waited.

"Lord, I am a man who has lived many years, thinking greatly, but doing little-little. My own brother is chief of K'mana and has a medal about his neck, and men say 'kwas' to his judgments. Now I, who am greater than he because of my thoughts, am only a common man. Tell me, Tibbetti, must all men be as they were born?"

Bones began to take an interest.

"Man, what is your name?" And when his visitor had told him: "M'gula, many men have been born common, but have come to greatness. That is well known."

Warming to his subject, and conscious of the improving character of his lecture, Bones became very voluble. He cited the story of a certain young Corsican officer of artillery who had reached for a throne; he told of a poverty-stricken boy in a rolling-mill ("a wonder of iron" he called him) who had acquired riches; he ransacked and misquoted history to preach the doctrine of opportunism, and M'gula of the Upper Ochori sat motionless, entranced.

"Now I see that you are wiser than M'Shimba, and greater than ghosts," he said, when Bones had talked himself out. "And I have a warm feeling in my stomach because I know that men become great from their thoughts."

He came again the next morning, and Bones, who in the meantime had raked up a few more historical instances, continued his discourse on Self-Help.

"The leopard comes once to the net" (thus he paraphrased the proverb of opportunity knocking at the door), "and if the net is fast, behold, he is your meat! But if the net is old and the pit is shallow, he goes and comes no more."

M'gula went back to the Ochori country an enlightened man.

A month after his return, his brother, the chief, was seized with a passionate desire to stand up before the people of his village and recite the poem called "M'sa." It is a poem by all standards, native or white, for it deals with death in a picturesque and imaginative way. There was not a man or a man-child from one end of the territory to the other who could not recite "M'sa" had he been so terribly defiant of devils and ju-jus. But it is the law that "M'sa" must be taught in whispers and in secret places from whence all birds have been frightened, for birds are notoriously members of the spirit world that carry news and chatter in their strange ways about the souls of men.

In a whisper must the poem be taught; in a whisper recited, and then the last word, which is "M'sa," must never be uttered. No man has ever explained what "M'sa" means. It is enough that it is so fearful a word that it sets men shivering even to think of it.

It is recorded that for a hundred years no man, sane or mad, had spoken "M'sa," so that when Busubu, the little chief of the Ochori, stood up by the village fire and, with some dramatic ability, recited the great poem in a tremendous voice, his people first sat frozen with horror at the sacrilege and its terrible significance, then broke and fled to their huts, hands to ears. In the night, when Busubu was sleeping, his two sons and his brother came to his hut and wakened him softly.

He rose and went with them into the forest, and they walked all night until they came to a big swamp where crocodiles laid their eggs. The waters of the pool rippled and swirled continuously in the grey light of dawn.

They rested by the side of a small lake, and the brother spoke.

"Busubu, you have brought upon the people the terrible Ghost who shall make us all slaves. This we know because our father told us. This ghost is chained by the leg at the bottom of this swamp, waiting for the words of 'M'sa' to reach him, when he shall be free. Now, I think, Busubu, you must speak to this spirit."

"O man and brother," whimpered Busubu the chief, "I would not have said the terrible words if you had not told me that it was the order of Sandi that I should do this. For did you not come secretly to my hut and say that Sandi had killed the ghost and that all men might say 'M'sa' without fear?"

"You are mad and a liar," said M'gula calmly. "Let us finish."

And because they would not have his blood on their hands, they roped him to a tree near by where the ripples ran most frequently, and they put out his eyes and left him. They rested awhile within earshot of the place, and when, in the afternoon, they heard certain sounds of pain, they knew that their work was consummated and went back to the village.

"Now, sons of Busubu," said the uncle of the young men, "if this matter goes to the ear of Sandi, he will come with his soldiers and we shall hang. Tomorrow let us call a full palaver of the people in this village, and all those countrymen who live in the forest, and tell them that Busubu was mad and fell into the river, and was drowned."

"His leg being caught by the terrible ones," suggested his nephew helpfully. "And, M'gula, I will sit in my father's place and give justice. When Sandi comes, and hearing me speak cleverly, he shall say: 'This son of Busubu is my chief.'"

His proposal aroused no enthusiasm.

"It is I who will sit in the place of my brother, for I am an old man, and old men are wise. And when Sandi comes I will speak for you both," he added cunningly.

And so it was arranged. M'gula sat on the stool of office on the thatched palaver house, and gave judgment and made speeches. One day he invited his two nephews to a great feast of fish and *manioc*. After the feast the young men were taken ill. They were buried in a middle island the next morning, and M'gula took their wives into his house. Bosambo, Paramount Chief of the Ochori, heard rumours, and sent a pigeon to Sanders a month or so later.

"M'gula? Who the devil is M'gula?" demanded Hamilton.

They were at breakfast in the big, airy dining-room of the residency. Sanders had read aloud a message that had come by pigeon post that morning.

7

"My dear old Ham!" said Bones, who sat opposite to him, "my *dear* Captain and Honourable! Do you mean to tell me that you don't know M'gula?"

Lieutenant Tibbets sat with coffee cup poised, an expression of incredulity and wonder on his pink face. He spoke a little thickly.

"I wish to heavens, Bones, you wouldn't speak with your mouth full. Weren't you taught manners as a boy?"

Bones swallowed something rapidly and painfully. "You've made me swallow a plum-stone, cruel old prefect," he said reproachfully. "But don't get off M'gula. I don't profess to know every jolly old indigenous native by sight, but I know M'gula – he's the fisherman johnny: quite a lad... Isisi river. Am I right, excellency?"

Sanders, lighting a black cheroot, shook his head. "You're wrong. He's a man of the Northern Ochori."

"When I said Isisi," said Bones shamelessly, "I naturally meant the Ochori. I know his father. Jolly nice, amiable old rascal..."

"I hanged his father ten years ago," said the patient Sanders, "and I think that hanging runs in the family."

"It does," murmured Bones, unabashed. "Now that you come to mention him, sir, I remember him. M'gula, of course. Dear old Ham, I'm really surprised at your forgetting a fellow like M'gula!"

"What has he been doing, sir?" asked Hamilton.

"Poison – that is certain; probably a more picturesque murder, though I think that is going to be difficult to prove. Busubu, the little chief in that part of the country, has disappeared. I think he was a little mad. The last time I was through the country he was developing sleep sickness – the neck glands were typical, but I thought he'd last longer before the mad stage was reached."

He tapped his white teeth with the tip of his fingers – evidence of his uneasiness.

"I've half a mind to send you up to the country, Bones – you could take the *Wiggle* and call in on Bosambo *en route*."

"Surely it is rather a simple matter to bring M'gula to trial?" asked Hamilton. "It isn't unusual. A chief mysteriously disappears, a relative jumps into the vacant place...?"

Sanders shook his head. "There is a curious feature about this crime – if it is a crime. Nobody can be found who can or will give evidence. Usually, even in a small village, you can collect a dozen stories that fit together. Bosambo says that two months ago M'gula made a journey to headquarters – I don't remember his coming."

Something in Bones' face attracted his superior's attention.

"Bones! You saw him?"

"Did I, dear old Ham? I'm blessed if I remember. What with sitting up all night with your jolly old hens – "

"You saw him, and I'll bet your infernal passion for educating the unfortunate native is responsible. What branch of study did you take?"

Bones rose from the table and folded his serviette deliberately.

"If every time a naughty old chief disappears you're going to lay it at my door, sir," he said bitterly, "and if every – " Suddenly he stopped and his tone changed. "What about sending me up to nose around, excellency? I don't want to praise myself, but I've got a gift for that sort of work. Things you wouldn't notice, dear old bat-eyed superior, I should spot in a minute. You know me, excellency – when you lost your cigarette holder, who found it?"

"I did," said Hamilton.

"But who put you on the track, dear old Ham? Who was it said, 'Did you look in your pocket?' Me! I bet I'd unearth this mystery in two twinks! It's observation that does it. A little bit of cigar ash, a torn-up letter. Things an ordinary johnny wouldn't think of looking for..."

"I don't think you'll find either cigar ash or letters in the Ochori forest," said Sanders drily, "but I do feel that this matter should be inquired into. Take the *Wiggle*, Bones, and go to the village. You might pick up Bosambo on your way. Leave the appointment of a new chief to him. And be careful! These folk of the north are queer and clannish. Even Bosambo has never quite mastered them. You may be successful."

Bones smiled indulgently at the word "may."

Bosambo, Paramount Chief of the Ochori, held a palaver of all his fifty chiefs, for there was trouble in the land. The crops had unexpectedly failed, goat sickness had made a mysterious and devastating appearance, and three considerable tribes had refused tribute, and had sent defiant messages to their lord. There was talk of a confederation between these, and that could only mean war. Moreover, a collector of taxes had been beaten to death, and another, Bosambo suspected, had been drowned. Bosambo, wearing his cloak of monkey tails and in his hand his three short killing spears, listened hour after hour as speaker after speaker arose and addressed him. Then at last spoke M'febi, a chief and suspected witch-doctor. All the day he had been waiting for this man, the most powerful of his subjects and the most antagonistic.

"Lord Bosambo, you have heard," said M'febi, in a deathly silence, "from one end of the land to the other there is sickness, and none who lie down at night know what the sun will show. Now I know, being a wise man and acquainted with mysteries, that there is a reason, and this I tell you. The Fearful Word has been spoken, and the Swamp Ghost is abroad."

A murmur of horror ran through the assembly. Men rubbed their hands in the dust and smeared their arms hurriedly.

"Because of this," M'febi went on, gratified by the sensation he had caused, "our crops are rotting and our goats lie down and die, making noises in their throats. Now you, Bosambo, who are so clever and are loved by Sandi, you shall show us a magic that will make the corn rise up and the goats become lively."

Bosambo raised his hand to check further eloquence.

"M'febi," he said, "am I a magician? Can I make the dead live? Say this."

M'febi hesitated, sensing danger. "Lord, you are not," he admitted.

"It was good you said that," said Bosambo ominously, "for if I were such a magician I should have speared you where you stand, knowing that I could bring you to life again. As for the Fearful Word, that is your story. And, I tell you, M'febi, that I have a quick way with men and chiefs who bring me ghosts when I ask for rubber. They also make noises in their throats and sleep on their faces. I will have tribute, for that is my due and the due of Sandi and his king. As for these northern men who conspire against me, I will take fire and spears to them, and they shall give blood for tribute. The palaver is finished."

That day he summoned his fighting regiments, young men who sneered at spirits and laughed in the face of M'shimba M'shamba Himself, and they came to the call of his *lokali*, in tens and tens from every village within sound of his drum, and made spear play on the plain beyond the city.

Bones arrived to find the capital an armed camp, and Bosambo, meeting him on the beach, thought it prudent to say nothing of the unrest in his land. It was when Bones put forward the suggestion that the chief should accompany him to the northern territory that his face fell, and he found some difficulty in explaining his unwillingness.

"Lord Tibbetti, I would go to the end of the world for Sandi, but for you I would go up into hell. But now is a bad time, for I have many palavers to hold, and it is the month of taxing. Therefore, Tibbetti, go alone, and I will come after you before the full moon."

A plan which suited the amateur detective, who wanted the full credit for the discoveries he was confident of making.

"This Busubu was mad," said Bosambo at parting. "As to M'gula, I know nothing of him because he is a common man. I think if you would burn his feet a little he would tell you, Tibbetti, for the soles of old men are very tender."

Bones knew a better way.

On the morning of the day that Bones arrived in the village, M'gula held a secret conference with the chiefs of the three revolting tribes, whose territories adjoined his own.

"My spies have brought me word that Tibbetti is coming with soldiers in his little ship to hear the manner of Busubu's death. Now, Tibbetti is my friend, for he has shown me the way to power. And because he is my friend, I will send him to you to make a palaver."

"But if he comes, he will bring his soldiers," demurred one of the rebel chiefs, "and that would be a bad palaver. How do we know, M'gula, that you will not speak evilly of us to Tibbetti, who is the son of Sandi? For it is clear that you have now become a man too great for your village, and they say that you desire to rule the three northern tribes in the manner of Gubala."

He named an ancient chief who had been dead 800 years, but to the native 800 years is yesterday, and yesterday is centuries past.

M'gula was nonplussed by the crude expression of his own secret thoughts and ambitions.

"After Tibbetti has gone, we will speak again," he said. "You shall come to my fine house and we will have a feast."

"Better you came to my fine house and had a feast," said the spokesman of the northern tribes, significantly, "for I do not wish to have a pain in my belly, and lie in the middle island, M'gula."

It seemed that the death of M'gula's nephews had not passed unnoticed. However, he appeased his guests, sent them back to their territories satisfied with his *bona fides*, and prepared for the coming of Bones.

Lieutenant Tibbetts had not arrived in the village more than half an hour before; with a large pipe in his mouth and a ferocious frown on his face, he began his investigations. Willing but untruthful men and women showed him the exact spot on the beach where Busubu had been standing when the crocodile seized him. In corroboration they pointed to the identical silurian, basking at that moment on a low sandbank in the middle of the river, open-mouthed. Bones had a momentary impulse to shoot the crocodile and make a thorough investigation of his interior, but thought perhaps that too long a time had passed for such clues to be of any value. With the assistance of a tape-measure and a piece of pencil he made an exact plan of the village, showing the distance from Busubu's house to the river. Then he interviewed Busubu's late wives, sullen, stupid women, wholly absorbed in their domestic occupations. They could tell him nothing except that Busubu had gone out of the hut and had not come back. They conveniently forgot the circumstances of his leaving. They only knew he did not return, and that they had gone into the house of M'gula.

"Very baffling," said Bones, shaking his head seriously.

He slept at night on the little steamer, which was moored close to the bank. His days were occupied in his search, his evenings in the acquirement of knowledge. If he could inspire M'gula, M'gula would tell him much that would fascinate him. Bones had a passion for native folklore, and learnt three new stories about snakes, a brand new legend concerning M'shimba M'shamba, and a mystery poem.

"Lord, this is the great secret of our people," said M'gula in a hushed voice; "for any man who knows this poem has power over all the world. And if it were known that I had taught you, I think my people would kill me. If a white lord speaks this wonder, all men will worship him, and he shall be as great as M'shimba. Because I love you, Tibbetti, and because you have told me so many beautiful things, I have taught you this. Now say with me again the words: 'Talaka m'sidi lulanga…' "

So Bones became word perfect. He had been a week conducting his investigations, without discovering anything more than he knew when he arrived; on the seventh day came an invitation from Lusingi.

"Lord, these people are in revolt against Bosambo, who has treated them cruelly. I think it would please Sandi if you spoke to them in your loving way, for they are very simple. Also, lord, if you spoke to them the poem which I have told you, they would be very worshipful, giving you the tribute which they deny to Bosambo."

It was an opportunity at which Bones jumped. To go back and confess his failure as a detective was one thing; to carry in his hands the pacification of a revolting tribe was another. Sanders would value the latter achievement even more than the unravelling of the mystery of Busubu's death.

The city of Lusingi lay five miles from the river, and Bones went gaily, unattended. M'gula walked with him to the end of the village street, and then returned with his counsellors.

"I think the people of Lusingi will kill Tibbetti," he said cheerfully, "and then I will send word to Sandi, and he will know I am his true friend, and give me the four tribes. In this way do men become great, Osuru, even as the lord Tibbetti said."

13

The innocent Bones reached the town and was met by the chief and escorted to the palaver house. Looking down on the mass of unfriendly faces that were turned up to him, Bones smirked inwardly.

Their grievances he knew. The uneasy chief, not knowing what military forces might be behind Tibbetti, had stated them concisely. There was a devil in the land, and goats were dying; and on the top of this, Bosambo had sent for his tribute – a familiar plaint.

"O people," said Bones, "I see you."

He spoke fluently in the soft and silky tongue of the Northern Ochori, which differs slightly from the Bomongo tongue used from one end of the river to the other.

"Sandi has sent me here to look into your hearts…"

His address mainly dealt with native economics. Here Bones was speaking as an expert, because he was well grounded in the problems which confronted these peasant farmers. Presently he came to his peroration.

"O people, hear me! I speak for Sandi, and for the Government. When the crops are good and your goats are many, and the little trees in the forest give you rubber in plenty, do you not make a store of corn and rubber, so that when the bad days come, you shall neither starve nor come empty-handed to your Paramount Chief? Now, these days have come, and your stores must be opened, and that which is buried must be dug up. This is the way of all the world, that bad days and good days follow one another."

His audience stared at him stonily. The miserly traits of the Northern Ochori are notorious.

"And now I will say to you a poem of great power and magic," said Bones, smacking his lips in anticipation. "Let all men listen…"

A silence as of the grave fell upon his audience with the first words of his great effort. Bones closed his eyes and started. He was thoroughly enjoying himself. He heard a rustle of movement, and drew an altogether wrong conclusion as to its cause. When he opened his eyes he was alone. The little hill, which had been covered thickly with the people of the town, was deserted. Men and women were flying to the shelter of their own homes, that their ears should not be shocked by the Fearful Word.

"Good Lord!" gasped Bones, and looked round.

The chief and his counsellors had already disappeared. He was entirely alone. In a few moments there was nothing human in sight, and the hair at the back of his neck lifted. Bones had smelt the danger instantly.

He drew his long-barrelled Browning from the holster at his side, felt for the spare magazine he always carried, and, pulling back the jacket of the pistol, pushed a cartridge into the chamber. Then he walked slowly down the hill. His way back to the river lay through the interminable main street of the town. Keeping to the centre of the broad road, he walked without haste, and from the dark interiors savage eyes followed him. And still there was no movement. Looking round, he glimpsed one head thrust out from an open doorway, but it was instantly withdrawn.

He knew that nothing would happen to him while he was in the town; the danger lay in the thick woods beyond. He put up his hands and measured the distance of the sun from the horizon. He had three-quarters of an hour before night fell, and he was five and a half miles from the boat.

It was the poem, he thought; and somehow he connected the poem with the mysterious disappearance of Busubu. Reaching the end of the village street, he walked quickly through the rank grass which separated him from the forest path.

Whizz!

A spear flew past him, buried itself in a tree, quivering. Bones spun round, his gun outstretched. There was nobody in sight.

Then he broke into a run, and instantly the spears began to fall around him. He located the point of attack: it was the long grass to the left. Levelling his pistol, he fired twice, and a dark figure sprang up and fell again. This time Bones really ran.

The path twisted and turned, with never more than a dozen straight yards; and so long as he could keep ahead of his pursuers, he was safe, for the wood was too thick for spear work. He padded on swiftly, but the sound of feet behind him grew nearer and nearer, and he stopped and turned. As he did so, the sound of the running ceased.

Bones could not afford to wait, for he knew that the men who were following him were at that moment moving through the forest from trunk to trunk, in an attempt to outflank him. Again he ran, and this time the hunters came into view. A spear passed so close to him that it brushed his gaitered leg.

Subconsciously he wondered how they came to miss him, for the Ochori are famous spearmen, and it was only later he learnt that the swamp demanded a live sacrifice. He turned and fired three times into the thick of his hunters and checked them for a second; then, as he thought he had reached an elbow of the path, a spear fell between his legs. He stumbled and fell, and before he could rise, they were on him. Near by was a crazy death-hut, one of the places to which the people of the town take their aged relatives when they are past work and are becoming a burden to the community. Here they die, and the wild beasts carry them to their lairs.

"This is a bad thing you do, man," said Bones when he recovered his breath; "for presently Sandi will come and then I think there will be many hangings."

He addressed the chief of Lusingi who had welcomed him less than an hour before.

"Tibbetti, though we all hang, you must die, for you have spoken the Fearful Word that loosens the great Ghost of the Swamp, and now misfortune will come to this land, and our children will have sickness, and fire will fall on our huts. Because we are afraid, we shall take you to the swamp of the Ghost, and we shall blind you a little, and afterwards the fearful ones will have you. So sleep, Tibbetti, for when the moon comes up we must walk."

They had taken away his arms, but they had not bound him, and Bones sat down on the floor of the hut, his head in his hands, considering the possibilities of escape. They were few, for it seemed that every man capable of carrying a spear had left the town and had come out to hunt him. From where he sat he could see that the wood was filled with men. The prospect was not cheerful.

Presently he saw the chief pass the entrance of the hut, and called him.

"Tell me," he said, "did Busubu speak the Fearful Word?"

The chief shook his head affirmatively.

"And thus he died, by the pool of the swamp!"

"Lord, thus he died," agreed the other.

"Mystery solved!" said Bones with melancholy satisfaction.

He had been up early that morning, and he had had an exhausting day. There was something in the suggestion which the chief had made. He was healthy and young and lived in the minute. He had hardly stretched himself upon the ground before he was asleep.

When Bones awoke it was daylight, and he sat up quickly. Through the opening of the hut there was nobody in sight. Something hanging on the thin roof-beam caught his eye and he gasped.

It was his belt and pistol.

"I'm dreaming," said Bones.

He went blinking out into the light. At the edge of the forest path were two trees, and a man was sitting, his back to Bones, gazing interestedly at two uncomfortable figures tied very tightly to the trunks.

"Bosambo!" called Bones sharply, and the watcher rose.

"Lord, I came up in the night, I and my young men, and M'gula showed me the way you had gone and told me of the Fearful Word he had made you speak."

"He told you...?"

Bosambo did not meet his eyes.

"Lord Tibbetti, you have the wisdom of a snake. This they told me in the village: that you measured many things with your fine ribbon and looked at many things through your glass-that-makes-little-things-into-big-things."

Bones went pink.

"Also by looking at leaves and cooking-pots and digging in the sand, and other cunning methods, you sought to find which way Busubu went. All this is very wonderful, but I am a simple man. I

17

burnt M'gula a little, and the soles of old men are very tender…and he told me."

★ ★ ★

"I knew all along that it was M'gula," said Bones to an admiring audience. "In the first place there was a patch of black mud, dear old officer, on the foot of his bed. That showed me two things – and this is where the jolly old art of deduction comes in – it showed me that he had come a long journey and – and – "

"That he'd been standing in mud," said Hamilton helpfully.

"Exactly!" said the triumphant Bones. "Where did the mud come from?"

"From mud," suggested Hamilton.

Bones clicked his lips impatiently.

"Dear old officer! Let me tell the story, *please* – that is, if you want to hear it."

"I'm afraid, Bones, you've been forestalled – Bosambo has sent me two very long and detailed messages," smiled Sanders. "According to him, M'gula confessed under a primitive form of torture."

Only for a second was Bones nonplussed.

"But who was it set his jolly old conscience working?" he demanded in triumph.

THE MEDICAL OFFICER OF HEALTH

For the use of Mr Augustus Tibbetts, Lieutenant of Houssas, and called by all and sundry "Bones," a hut had at one time been erected. It was a large hut, and in many ways a handsome hut, and would have accommodated 999 young officers out of a thousand. There was even a shower bath operating from a lofty barrel. But the interests of Bones were multifarious. His hobbies were many. They came and went, and in their passing left on the shelves, in the cupboards and under the table and bed, distinct evidence of their existence. As the scientist may, by the examination of geological strata, trace the history of the world, so might an expert delving into the expensive litter of his hutment, follow Bones from the Devonian eras (represented by a passionate search for rare and remarkable stamps) through Cretaceous, Tertiary, and Quarternary strata of study and recreation.

Another hut had been added to store his collection, and on its native-built shelves reposed old wireless sets that did not work and never had worked, volumes of self-improvers, piles of literature, thousands of samples ranging from linoleum to breakfast foods, boxes of scientific and quasi-scientific instruments (he took a correspondence course in mountain railway construction, although there were no mountains nearer than Sierra Leone), and rolls of electric flexes.

"What an infernal junk shop!" said Hamilton appalled.

He had come over to make a few caustic remarks about the key of the store-house which, as usual when Bones had its temporary

19

custody, had been left all night in the door, thereby offering temptation to Hamilton's Houssas, who were loyal but dishonest.

"To your unscientific eyes, my dear old captain and comrade, yes," said Bones quietly. "To my shrewd old optics, no. Everything there has its value, its *raison d'être* – which is a French expression that is Greek to you, dear old Ham – its – its requirability."

"What is this?" asked Hamilton, picking up a queer-looking object.

"That," said Bones without hesitation, "is an instrument used in wireless – it would take too long to explain, Ham. Unless you've got a groundin' in science, dear old ignoramus, any explanation would be undecipherable – "

"Unintelligible is the word you want," said Hamilton, and read with difficulty the words stamped upon the steel side of the instrument. " 'Robinson's Patent Safety Razor Strop' – you don't mean 'wireless' – you mean 'hairless.' "

"I wish to good gracious heavens you wouldn't mess things about," said Bones testily, as he fixed his monocle and glared at the unoffending strop.

"The truth is, Bones," said Hamilton when he reached the open and had drawn in long draughts of air with offensive ostentation, "you ought to burn all that rubbish. You'll be breeding disease of some kind."

Bones closed his eyes and raised his eyebrows.

"I am fightin' disease, dear old layman," he said gravely, and, going back to the hut, returned with a large wooden box. Holding this in the cross of his arm, he opened the lid and disclosed, lying between layers of cotton wool, a number of long, narrow, wooden cases.

"Good Lord!" gasped Hamilton in dismay. "Are *you* going to do it?"

Bones nodded even more gravely.

"When did this come – Sanders told me nothing about it?"

A faint and pitying smile dawned on the angular face of Bones.

"There are some things which our revered old excellency never tells anybody," he said gently. "You have surprised our secret, dear old Ham – may I ask you, as a man of honour an' sensibility, dear old Peepin' Tom, not to mention the fact that I have told you? I trust you."

Hamilton went back to the residency, and, in defiance of the demand for secrecy, mentioned his discovery.

Mr Commissioner Sanders looked up from his work. "Vaccination lymph? Oh yes, it came this morning, and I sent it over to Bones. We may not want it, but Administration is worried about the outbreak in the French territory, and it may be necessary to inoculate the border people. Bones had better take charge – they can't spare a doctor from HQ."

"God bless the lad!" said Hamilton in great relief. "I was afraid that I should be the goat."

Sanders nibbled the end of his penholder. "Bones has imagination, and I think he will want it when he comes to tackle the Lesser Isisi folk."

"He certainly is a ready liar," admitted Hamilton.

Government departments have a mania for labelling any man who occupies, temporarily or permanently, a post under their directions. There is this sense in the practice – an official so labelled may be easily identified by the most obtuse of clerks. He may occupy a separate drawer in a filing cabinet, and to him, by reason of his labelling, may be attached responsibilities which fall within the designation they have found for him. Sanders received a wire from headquarters – the wire had been working without interruption for a month owing to the elephants, who have a playful habit of uprooting the poles moving inland for the breeding season, and the message ran:

"No. 79174. Administration H. Re your wire No. 531 T. Lt A Tibbetts, King's Houssas, is appointed temporary Health Officer and Sanitary Inspector your territories, with additional pay three shillings per diem as from 4th instant until further notice. He will indent and report under letters HO and S1. Acknowledge."

Sanders duly acknowledged and communicated the momentous news to his subordinate. Bones received the intelligence very gravely.

"Of course, dear old excellency, I shall do my best," he said seriously. "The responsibility is simply fearful."

Thereafter, to use Hamilton's own expressive language, life became simply Hell.

At breakfast, Bones invariably came late, smelling strongly of disinfectant, his manner subdued, his tone severely professional.

"Good morning, excellency...Ham – Ham!"

"What the devil's the matter with you?" demanded the startled Ham.

"Have you washed your hands, dear old officer?"

"That's sunburn, you jackass!"

Bones shook his head. "Use a weak solution of carbolic acid, dear old infectious one," he murmured. "Can't be too careful in these days."

He invariably carried a sheet of white paper, which he laid on the chair before he sat down, and he insisted upon a cup of boiling-hot water being placed on the table so that he might sterilise his fork and knife.

When, one morning, Sanders came into breakfast and found the dining-room reeking with carbolic, he struck.

"Bones, I appreciate your conscientious efforts on behalf of hygiene, but if you don't mind, I'd rather die of disease than endure this stink."

"Microbes, dear old excellency," murmured Bones. "This is stuff that makes naughty old Mike go red in the face."

"I prefer that he remains pale," said Sanders, and called his orderly to open the windows.

More annoying was the practice which Bones initiated of inspecting his superiors' sleeping quarters. Hamilton found him in his bedroom with a tape measure and a look of profound distress.

"Ham, old fugg-wallah, this won't do at all!" said Bones, shaking his head reprovingly. "Bless my jolly old life and soul, you'd be *dead* if I hadn't come in! How many cubic feet do you think you've got?"

"I've got two feet," answered the exasperated Hamilton, "and if you're not out of this room in three twinks, I'm going to use one of them!"

"And what's all this?" Bones stirred a heap of clothing with the end of his stick. "Trousers, dear old thing, coats an' hats – don't get peevish, Ham. Us medical lads – "

" 'Us' ," sneered Hamilton. "You illiterate hound! Get out!"

It is very trying to be brought into daily and hourly contact with a man who smelt alternately of lysol and naphthaline. It was maddening to find dinner delayed because Bones had strolled into the kitchen and had condemned the cooking arrangements; but the culmination of his infamy came when he invented a new filter that turned the drinking water a deep, rich pink that made it taste of iron filings.

"Can't you telegraph to headquarters and have him reduced to the ranks, sir?" asked Hamilton savagely, after he had found crystals of pure carbolic acid in his shaving mug. "I'm being sanitised to death!"

Happily a tax-collecting tour was due, and Sanders was not sorry. Bones, of course, ordered the thorough fumigation of the *Zaire*, and for three days after the little steamer started on her voyage, the unhappy crew breathed sulphur fumes and drank sulphur water and ate sulphurated rice.

Bones came down to the quay, a strange and awesome spectacle; a thin veil of antiseptic gauze hung from the edges of his helmet like a curtain, and on his hands were odorous gloves.

"Hail to the bride!" snarled Hamilton from the bridge. "Where's your orange blossom, Birdie?"

"I order you to keep away from the Ochori," cried Bones in a muffled voice. "There's measles there – drink nothing but Lithia water..."

Hamilton replied offensively.

* * *

There runs between the Pool of the Silent Ones and the Lesser Isisi, a strip of land which is neither forest nor swamp, and yet is of the nature of both. Here grow coarse trees that survive even the parasitical growths which shoot upward in one humid night to the height of a tall man; and here come the silent ones to sleep between trees, secure in the swamps that surround them and the guardianship of those little birds who love crocodiles and stand sentinel over them when they slumber. Of other birds there are few; other beasts do not come to the Wood of the Waters, and the elephants' playing ground is on the firmer shore of the river. Here they have levelled the trees and stamped the earth flat, so that they may gambol and chase one another, and the calves may fight to the applause of trumpetings and waving trunks. There are many rotting huts in the Wood of the Waters, for the Isisi send here the old, the blind, and the mad, that they may die without distressing the whole and the sane. Sometimes they kill one another, but generally a scaly form creeps up from the mud and knocks them into the water with its quick tail, and there is an end.

Mr Commissioner Sanders was mad, but not slayable, by reason of his soldiers, his long-nosed "wung-wung" (so they called his hotchkiss) and the brass-jacketted guns that said "ha-ha-ha!"

Nobody but a madman would go squelching through the noisome mud of the wood, peering into foul huts, raking over ground for signs of skeletons (all that the crocodiles did not take was the little red ants' by right). Yet this is what Sandi did. He slowed his fine boat and brought her to the bank.

"I have impressed upon Lulaga the impropriety of hastening the deaths of his relatives," he said to Captain Hamilton of the Houssas, "and he has sworn by M'shimba and his own particular devil that there shall be no more blinding or old-age pensioning," he added grimly.

Hamilton smiled wearily. " 'The customs of the country must not be lightly overridden or checked,' " he quoted from a famous Instruction received from the Colonial Office in bygone days – there isn't a Commissioner from K'sala to Tuli Drift who cannot recite it by heart, especially after dinner.

" 'Nor,' " he went on, " 'should his religious observances or immemorial practices be too rudely suppressed, remembering that the native, under God's providence, is a man and a brother.' "

24

"Shut up!" snarled Sanders, but the inexorable Houssa was not to be suppressed.

" 'He should be approached gently,' " he went on, " 'with arguments and illustrations obvious to his simple mind. Corporal punishment must under no circumstances be inflicted save in exceptionally serious crimes, and then only by order of the supreme judiciary of the country − ' "

"That looks to me like a new hut," said Sanders, and stepped over the hastily rigged gangway, twirling a mahogany stick in his thin, brown hand.

Threading his way through a green and anaemic plantation, he came to the hut, and there he found B'saba, sometime headman of the village of M'fusu, and B'saba was mad and silly and was chuckling and whimpering alternately, being far gone in sleeping sickness, which turns men into beasts. He was blind, and he had not been blind very long.

The nose of Sandi *elaka* wrinkled.

"O man, I see you, but you cannot see me. I am Sandi, who gives justice. Now tell me, who brought you here?"

"Lulaga the king," said the old man woefully. "Also he has taken my pretty eyes."

He died that night, Sanders squatting on the ground by his side and feeding the fire that warmed him. And they buried him deep, and Sanders spoke well of him, for he had been a faithful servant of Government for many years.

In the dawn-grey he turned the nose of the *Zaire* against the push of the black waters and came to the village of the chief, to that man's uneasiness.

The *lokalis* beat a summons to a great palaver, and in the reed-roofed hut Sanders sat in judgment.

"Lord!" said the trembling Lulaga. "I did this because of a woman of mine who was mocked by the old man in his madness."

"Let her come here," said Sanders, and they brought her, a mature woman of sixteen, very slim, supple and defiant.

"Give me your medal, Lulaga," said Sanders, and the chief lifted the cord that held his silver medal of chieftainship. And when Sanders had placed it upon the neck of a trustworthy man, and this man had eaten salt from the palm of the Commissioner's hand, soldiers tied Lulaga to a tree, and one whipped him twenty times across the shoulders, and the whip had nine tails, and each was a yard in length.

"Old men and madmen shall die in good time," said Sanders. "This is the law of my King, and if this law be broken I will come with a rope. Hear me! The palaver is finished."

There came to him, as he made his way back to the ship, an elderly man who, by the peculiar shape of his spear, he knew was from the inner lands.

"Lord, I am M'kema of the village by the Frenchi," he said, "being a chief of those parts. Now, it seems to me that you have taken away the magic which our fathers gave to us, for all men know that the sick and old are nests where devils breed, and unless we kill them gently there will be sickness in the land. On the other side of the little river the Frenchi people are very sick, and some say that the sickness will come to us. What magic do you give us?"

Sanders was instantly alert.

"Any men of the Frenchi tribes who cross the river you shall drive back with your spears," he said, "and if they will not go, you shall kill them and burn their bodies. And I will send Tibbetti, who carries many wonders in a little box, so that you shall not be harmed."

On the way down river, Sanders was unusually thoughtful. Not less so was Captain Hamilton, for, as the elder man had said, from the beginning of time every tribe, save the Ochori, had carried its ancient men and women into the forest and left them there to die. Sanders had threatened; he had on occasions caught men in the act of carrying off their uncomfortable relatives; but never before had he punished so definitely for a custom which the ages had sanctioned.

They smelt headquarters before they saw the grey quay and the flowering palm-tops that hid the residency. Suddenly Sanders sniffed.

"What in the name of Heaven – !" he asked.

A gentle wind, blowing in from the sea, carried to him a strange and penetrating odour. It was not exactly the smell of tar, nor was it the scent which one associates with a burning soap factory. It combined the pungent qualities of both. Later, Sanders learnt that, in his absence, a trading steamer had called and had landed half-a-dozen carboys of creosote for the use of the Health Officer, and that Bones, in his enthusiasm and in that capacity, had tried the experiment of a general fumigation. The fire whereon the creosote had been transformed into its natural gases, still smouldered in the centre of the square, and Bones, a fearsome object in a gas mask, and without any assistance – his men had practically mutinied and flown to their huts – was continuing the experiment when, in sheer self-defence, Sanders pulled the siren of the *Zaire* and emitted so blood-curdling a yell that it reached beyond the protective covering of Bones' mask.

"For the love of Mike, what are you trying to do?" gasped Hamilton, spluttering and coughing.

Bones made signs. After his helmet had been removed, he propounded the results of his experiments.

"There isn't a jolly old rat left alive," he said triumphantly; "the beetles have turned in their jolly old numbers, and the mosquitos have quietly passed away!"

"Are any of the company left?" demanded Hamilton. "Phew!"

"Creosote," began Bones, in his professorial manner, "is one of those jolly old bug-haters – "

"Bones, I've got a job for you," said Sanders hastily. "Get steam in the *Wiggle* and go up to the Lesser Isisi and on to the French frontier. Near a village which I gather is M'taka there is smallpox. Vaccinate everybody within a ten mile radius and be happy."

"And keep away from the French territory," warned Hamilton.

Bones smiled contemptuously. "Am I a ravin' old ass?"

"Not 'old,' " said Hamilton.

Within two hours Bones was on his way, a huge pipe clenched between his teeth, a pair of horn-rimmed spectacles ("And God knows where he got those from!" said Hamilton in despair) on his nose, and, balanced upon his knees, a ponderous medical tome. The fact that it was a surgical work dealing with nerve centres made no difference to Bones, it was the only medical work he had – it had been sent to him, in response to his written request to a London publisher for a novel that was enjoying some popularity at the time. And if, reading Bones' vile handwriting, the publisher translated his request for "Walter Newman's Sister" into "Watts' Diseases of the Nervous System," he was hardly to blame.

In course of time he came to the Lesser Isisi, and was received with great honour by the new chief. It seemed that every man, woman and child in the village had turned out to meet him. But there were no marks of special enthusiasm, nor did any of the people smile. And the folk of the Lesser Isisi are only too ready to laugh.

"Lord," said the new chief, "all men know that you bring great magic in your two hands, for Sandi has spoken well of you, and it is known that you are a friend of ju-jus and ghosts. Therefore, my people have come that they may see this magic which is greater than the magic of our fathers."

This he said publicly, for all men to hear. In the privacy of his hut, he told another story.

"The people have anger in their stomachs, because Sandi whipped Lulaga, and there have been secret palavers," he said. "And, lord, I think they will make an end to me. Also, there is a saying that Sandi loves death and hates the people of the Isisi, so that he would be glad if the cooking-pots were broken and the roofs of the village were fallen."

Thus he symbolised death, for when a man of the Isisi passes, the pots wherein his food was cooked are broken on his grave, and no man tends his hut until the winds and the rain bring it sagging to the ground.

"That is foolish talk," said Bones, "since Sandi has sent me to make all people well by the wonder which is in my little box. Behold, I will put into their arms a great medicine, so that they shall laugh at ghosts and mock at devils. For I am very honoured in my land because of my great wisdom with medicine," added Bones immodestly.

Accompanied by four soldiers, he marched two days into the forest and came at last to the village by the water, and arrived only in time;

for, in defiance of Sandi's orders, three men from the Frenchi village had crossed in the night and were being entertained by the headman himself. They left hurriedly and noisily, Bones chasing them to their canoe, and whacking at them with his walking stick until they were out of reach of his arm. Then he came back to the village and called a palaver. In the palaver house, placed upon an upturned drum, and covered with one of his famous sanitary handkerchiefs, were innumerable little tubes and a bright lancet.

"O people," said Bones in his glib Bomongo – and he spoke the language like a native – "Sandi has sent me because I am greater than ju-jus and more wonderful than devils. And I will put into your bodies a great magic, that shall make the old men young and the young men like leopards, and shall make your women beautiful and your little children stronger than elephants!"

He held up a tube of lymph, and it glittered in the strong sunlight.

"This magic I found through my wonderful mind. It was brought to me by three birds from M'shimba M'shamba because he loves me. Come you M'kema."

He beckoned the chief, and the old man came forward fearfully.

"All ghosts hear me!" said Bones oracularly, and his singsong voice had the quality of a parrot's screech. "M'shimba M'shamba, hear me! Bugulu, eater of moons and swallower of rivers, hear me!"

The old man winced as the lancet scraped his arm.

"Abracadabra!" said Bones, and dropped the virus to the wound.

"Lord, that hurts," said M'kema. "It is like the fire of Hell!"

"So shall your heart be like fire, and your bones young, and you shall skip over high trees, and have many new wives," promised Bones extravagantly.

One by one they filed past him, men, women and children, fear and hope puckered in their brows, and Bones recited his mystic formula.

They were finished at last, and Bones, weary but satisfied, went to the hut which had been prepared for him, and, furiously rejecting the conventional offer of the chief's youngest daughter for his wife – Sanders had a polite and suave formula for this rejection, but Bones invariably blushed and spluttered – went to sleep with a sense of having conferred a great blessing upon civilisation; for by this time Bones had forgotten that such a person as Dr Jenner had ever existed, and took to himself the credit for all his discoveries.

He spent an exhilarating three days in the village, indulging in an orgy of condemnation which would have reduced the little township to about three huts, had his instructions been taken literally. Then, one morning, came the chief, M'kema.

"Lord," he said, "there is a devil in my arm, and your magic is burning terribly. Now, I have thought that I will not have your magic, for I was more comfortable as a plain man. Also my wives are crying with pain, and the little children are making sad noises."

Walking down the village street, Bones was greeted with scowling faces, and from every hut, it seemed, issued moans of distress. In his wisdom Bones called a palaver, and his four soldiers stood behind him, their magazines charged, their rifles lying handily in the crooks of their unvaccinated arms.

As a palaver, it was not a success. He had hardly begun to speak before there arose a wail from his miserable audience, and the malcontents found a spokesman in one Busubu, a petty chief.

"Lord, before you came we were happy, and now you have put fiery snakes in our arms, so that they are swollen. Now by your magic make us well again."

And the clamour that followed the words drowned anything that Bones had to say. That night he decided to make his way back to the river.

He came from his hut and found Ahmet waiting for him.

"Lord, there is trouble here," said the Kano boy in a low voice, "and the young men have taken their spears to the forest path."

This was serious news, and a glance showed Bones that the village was very much awake. To force his way through the forest path was suicidal; to remain was asking for a six-line obituary notice in the *Guildford Herald*. Bones brought his party to the little river, and half the ground had not been covered before he was fighting a rear-guard action. With some difficulty they found a canoe, and paddled into midstream, followed by a shower of spears, which wounded one of his escort. In a quarter of an hour Bones stepped ashore at the Frenchi village, which turned out even at that late hour to witness such an unusual spectacle as the arrival of a British officer on alien soil.

He slept in the open that night, and in the morning the chief of the Frenchi village came to him with a complaint.

"Lord, when three of my men went over the M'taki, you whipped them so that they stand or sleep on their bellies. And this you did because of our famous sickness. Now, tell me why you sit down here with us, for my young men are very hot for chopping you."

"Man," said Bones loftily, "I came with magic for the people of the Lower Isisi."

"So it seems," said the French chief significantly, "and their magic is so great that they will give me ten goats for your head; yet because I fear Saudi I will not do this thing," he added hastily, seeing the Browning in Lieutenant Tibbetts' hand.

Briefly but lucidly, Bones explained the object of his visit, and the chief listened, unconvinced.

"Lord," he said at last, "there are two ways by which sickness may be cured. The one is death, for all dead men are well, and the other is by chopping a young virgin when the moon is in a certain quarter and the river is high. Now, my people fear that you have come to cure them by making their arms swell, and I cannot hold them."

Bones took the hint, and, re-embarking, moved along the little river till he came to another Isisi village. But the *lokali* had rapped out the story of his mission, and locked shields opposed his landing.

The chief of this village condescended to come to the water's edge.

"Here you cannot land, Tibbetti," he said, "for this is the order of Saudi to M'kema, that no man must come to us from the Frenchi land because of the sickness that is there."

For seven days and seven nights Bones was marooned between bank and bank, sleeping secretly at nights on such middle islands as he met with, and at the end of that time returned to the point of departure. M'kema came down to the beach.

"Lord, you cannot come here," he said, "for since you have gone the arms of my young men have healed owing to the magic of their fathers."

That night, when Bones had decided upon forcing a passage to the big river, the relief from the *Zaire* fought its way into the village and left him a clear path. Bones went back in triumph to headquarters and narrated his story.

"And there was I, dear old thing, a martyr, so to speak, to jolly old science, standing, as it were, with my back to the wall. I thought of jolly old Jenner – "

"Where were you, Bones? I can't quite place your defence," said Hamilton, peering over a map of the territory. "Were you in M'kema's village?"

"No, sir, I skipped," said Bones in triumph. "I went across the river to – "

Hamilton gasped. "Into the French territory?"

"It's a diplomatic incident, I admit," said Bones, "but I can explain to the President exactly the motives which led me to violate the territory of a friendly power – or, at least, they were not so friendly either, if you'd seen the 'Petit Parisienne' that came out by the marl – "

"But you were in the French village? That is all I want to know," said Hamilton with deadly quiet.

"I certainly was, old thing."

"Come with me," said Hamilton.

He led the way to Bones' hut and opened the door.

"Get in, and don't come near us for a month," he said. "You're isolated!"

"But, dear old thing, I'm Health Officer!"

"Tell the microbes," said Hamilton.

And isolated Bones remained. Every morning Hamilton came with a large garden syringe, and sprayed the ground and the roof thereof with an evil-smelling mixture. And, crowning infamy of all, he insisted upon handing the unfortunate Bones his meals through the window at the end of a long bamboo pole.

The Health Officer had come out of isolation, and had ceased to take the slightest interest in medical science, devoting his spare time to a new architectural correspondence course, when M'kema, summoned to headquarters, appeared under escort and in irons, to answer for his sins.

"Lord, Tibbetti did a great evil, for he took our people, who were well, and made them sick. Because their arms hurt them terribly they tried to chop him."

Sanders listened, sitting in his low chair, his chin on his fist.

"You are an old man and a fool," he said. "For did not the sickness come to the Isisi? And did not the villagers have their mourning – all except yours, M'kema, because of the magic which Tibbetti had put into their arms? Now, you are well, and the other villagers have their dead. How do you account for that, M'kema?"

M'kema shook his head. "Lord," he said, "it was not by the magic of Tibbetti, for he made us ill. We are well people, and the sickness passed us because we followed the practice of our fathers, and took into the forest a woman who was very old and silly, and, putting out her eyes, left her to the beasts. There is no other magic like this."

"What's the use?" asked the despairing Sanders, and M'kema, hearing these words in English, shivered, suspecting a new incantation.

THE BLACK EGG

There is a new legend on the river, and it is the legend of a devil who came from a black egg and hated its new master so powerfully that it slew him.

Once upon a time in the Isisi land, the birds ceased suddenly from gossiping at the very height of day, and goats and dogs stood up on their feet and looked uneasily from left to right, and there was in the world a sudden and an inexplicable hush, so that men came out of their huts to discover what was the matter.

And whilst they were so standing, gaping at a silence which was almost visible, the world trembled, and down the long street of the Isisi city came a wave and a billowing of earth, so that houses shook and men fell on to their knees in their fear. Then came another tremble and yet another billowing of solid ground, and the waters of the big river flowed up in sudden volume and flooded the lower beaches and washed even into the forest, which had never seen the river before.

Between the first and the second shocks of the earthquake, N'shimba was born, and was named at a respectful distance after that ghost of ghosts – more nearly after one who had been as terrible. M'shimba M'shamba notoriously dwelt in the bowels of the earth, and was prone to turn in his sleep.

Down the river went three canoes laden with wise men and chiefs, and they came solemnly into the presence of Mr Commissioner Sanders, who, in addition to being responsible for the morals and welfare of a few millions of murderous children predisposed to cannibalism, was regarded as a controller of ghosts, ju-jus, the incidence of rainfall and the fertility of crops.

"O Sandi, I see you," said M'kema, chief of the deputation. "We are poor men who have come a long journey to tell you of terrible happenings. For you are our father and our mother and you are very wise."

It was a conventional opening, and Sanders, who had felt the earthquake, an infrequent occurrence in these parts, waited, knowing what would come.

"...and then, lord, the river rose fearfully, washing through the huts of Bosubo, the fisherman, and eating up his salt. And the roof of Kusu, the hunter, fell down whilst he was in bed, and also two canoes were washed away and found by the thieving Akasava, who will not give them to us. Now tell us, Sandi, what made the world rock? Some of my councillors think one thing, some another. One says that it was M'shimba putting up his knees as he slept. Men do this in their sleep, as I know. Another, that it was a fight between two mighty ghosts. Speak for us, Sandi."

Sanders was not prepared to give a lecture on seismology, but supplied a plausible, fairly accurate, not wholly fanciful explanation.

"M'kema," said he, "in this world what do you see? The earth and the trees upon it, and the rivers that run on the earth. And if you dig, there is more earth. And if you dig deeper, there is rock and more rock, and beneath that – who knows? Sands and rivers and soft earth again. And if the rivers wash away the under earth, then the rocks settle and the ground settles, and there are strange disturbances. As to ghosts, I know M'shimba M'shamba, for he is my friend and well liked by the Government. But when he comes it is with a mighty wind and rains and spittings of fire. He lifts big trees and little trees and carries away huts, and he roars with a loud voice."

"*Cala cala*," said a grey wise man (Foliti, suspected of witchcraft), "in the days of our fathers this thing happened, and there was born in the midst of the wonder, a man whose name was Death."

Sanders knew the legend of the ancient N'shimba, and had fixed the date of his appearance at somewhere in the seventeenth century. This N'shimba, so miraculously born, had been a common man who had no respect for kings or authorities, and by his genius had made himself master of the land between the mountains and the sea. It was said that when he was a youth, a ghost brought him a black egg, and from this egg was hatched a devil, who gave him power so that he was greater than kings.

"This I know," he said. "Why do you say this to me, wise man?"

"Lord, such a child has now been born in our village, and the mother, being mad, has named him N'shimba. And doing this, she made strange faces and died, as the mother of N'shimba of our fathers died. Because of this we have held a palaver for three days and three nights. And some said that the baby must be buried alive before the ghost comes which will give him power, and some that he must be put in the Pool of the Silent Ones, and others that he must be chopped and all of us must put our fingers in his blood and smear the soles of our feet, this being magic."

Sanders wrinkled his nose like an angry terrier.

"Do this," he said unpleasantly, "and be sure that I will come with a magic rope and hang the men who chopped him. Go back, men, to your villages and let this be known. That I will send a Jesus-man to this child, and he shall take away all that is evil in him, and then will I come and fix to his forehead a certain devil mark which shall be strange to see. Thereafter let no man raise his hand against N'shimba, for my spirit will be powerfully with him. *Elaka!*"

Two days after a missionary had formally baptised N'shimba, Sanders came, and in view of all the silent village, pressed a small rubber stamp on the squirming baby's forehead. It was the stamp that Sanders used when he sent microscope slides to the School of Tropic Medicines for examination, and it said: "Fragile: open carefully."

In a sense it was an appropriate inscription.

"People, I have put my ju-ju upon this child," said Sanders, addressing the multitude. "Presently it will fade and go away, because by my magic it will eat into his bones and into his young heart. But because my magic is so fearful, I shall know who laid his hand upon this small one, and I shall come swiftly with my soldiers and my gun that says 'ha–ha–ha.' "

Such was the potency of the charm that, after many years, a slightly mad woman who struck the child, died in great agony the same night.

All this happened *cala cala*, in the days when Sanders was mapping out the destinies of five contentious nations. From time to time he saw the boy, and discovered in him nothing remarkable, except that he was a little sulky, and, according to his father, given to long silences and to solitary walks. He knew none of his own kind; neither played with boys nor spoke frankly to girls. They said that he was looking for the black egg, and certainly N'shimba climbed many trees without profit.

Then one day, N'shimba, squatting about the family fire before the hut, propounded a riddle.

"I caught a young leopard and put him in the fine little house, where once I had kept many birds. Did my leopard sing or fly or make 'chip–chip' noises?"

"Boy, you are foolish," said his unimaginative father, "for you have caught no leopard and you have no fine house where birds are kept."

"That is my mystery," said N'shimba, and, rising, walked away to the forest and was not seen for three days. When he returned, he brought with him a young girl of the Inner Isisi.

"This is my wife," he said.

The father said nothing, for the boy was sixteen and of a marrying age. The new wife, on the contrary, said much.

"I do not want this man, your son," she said frankly. "I am a great dancer, and my price is ten bundles of ten malakos in ten heaps ten times ten repeated. A man of my people would give as much salt as would fill a hut if I would be his wife, yet your son comes to me and takes me and gives nothing to my father nor to me. And when I turned from him, he struck me down. Here is the mark."

The mark was horridly patent, and N'shimba's father was troubled and sought his son.

"Why have you taken this woman?" he asked. "Presently her father will come and demand her price. And Sandi will come and give

37

judgment against me. Let her go, for, even if you are married to her, what does it matter? Is there not a saying that 'Women marry many times but have one husband'?"

"I am that man," said N'shimba. "As to Sandi, I am the child of his spirit, as all people know, and I take what I need."

That evening he beat his new wife, and her father, arriving in wrath to make the best of a bad bargain, was also beaten to his shame.

"Who is N'shimba?" asked Captain Hamilton curiously when the news came to headquarters, and Sanders, a thoughtful, troubled man, explained.

"It wouldn't worry me at all, but the young devil has used the slogan of the old N'shimba, 'I take what I need' – and that is a very bad sign. One whisper of black eggs and I will take N'shimba and hang him."

He sent a warning, and marked down N'shimba in his diary as one to be interviewed when he next went north. Then one day there came into existence the Blood Friends of Young Hearts.

In native territories, secret societies are born in a night, and with them their inspired ritual. From what brain they come, none knows. The manner of their dissolution is as mysterious. They come and they go; perform strange rites, initiate secret dances; men meet one another and say meaningless but thrilling words; there is a ferment and thrill in life – then of a sudden they are no more. Sometimes there is a little blood-letting, as when the N'gombi people held a society which was called The Mystery of the Five Straight Marks. Five cuts on the left cheek was the sign of the order. Sanders heard, saw, said nothing. On the whole, he thought the personal appearance of the N'gombi people was improved by the mutilations. But when, at a big palaver of the society, an Ochori girl was beheaded and her skin distributed to the members of the order, Sanders went quickly to the spot, hanged the leaders, flogged their headmen, and burnt the village that had been the scene of the ceremony. Thereafter the Five Marks vanished from existence.

"Ahmet says N'shimba is behind this new society," he said, calling Hamilton into his airy little office. "I'm scared lest N'shimba discovers that the mantle of his disreputable namesake has descended upon him. If he does, there will be bad trouble. I think I'll send Bones to the Isisi with a platoon of young men. The wholesome presence of authority may nip in the bud the activities of the Young Hearts."

"Why 'Young Hearts'?" asked Hamilton lazily.

"They are mostly young men, and the movement is spreading," said Sanders. "Bosambo has reported that a branch of this interesting society has been formed in the heart of the Ochori city."

"Send Bones," suggested Hamilton promptly. "I know of no more depressing influence."

"What is the matter with him!"

"If this were a civilised country, and the necessary opportunities existed, I should say that Bones was in love," said Hamilton. "As it is, I think he's sickening for something."

"It can't be measles," said Sanders. "He's had them twice."

Hamilton sniffed. "Bones is the sort of fellow who would have measles three times and never turn a hair. But it isn't measles. And it isn't liver. I had him in yesterday morning and insisted on his swallowing three pills. He made a fuss about it, and I had to quote the Army Act. And even now he's depressed."

Sanders stared thoughtfully across the sunburnt parade ground.

"I think a trip to the Isisi might do him a lot of good," he said.

★ ★ ★

There were moments when there came to the soul of Lieutenant Augustus Tibbetts a great unrest. Times when even the pursuit and practice of his latest course of study brought neither peace nor consolation. Bones (for such was his name to his equals) found a melancholy satisfaction in the phenomena, for these conditions of unease usually preceded some flashing inspiration. It was as though Nature in her mysterious way ordained that Bones should only put forth his finest efforts after some (to him) tremendous ordeal. Such a tinge of irritation came to Bones one sunny day in April, and at a moment when he had every reason to be perfectly happy. The mail had brought to him a diploma which certified to his proficiency as an accountant. He had been elected a Fellow of the Society of Accountancy (Wabash), as a result of a course of correspondence lessons conducted by The College of Practical and Theoretical Accountancy (also of Wabash, USA).

His half-yearly inspection had passed off magnificently, with the trifling exception that his books were out of order and that the sum of three pounds one shilling had in some mysterious fashion crept into the credit column. But this was instantly rectified by the discovery that he had added the day of the month, Bones invariably did this. Generally he added the year. Sometimes he was £192 1s short. Sometimes he had £19 2s 1d surplus. Sanders had praised some work of his; his immediate superior, Captain Hamilton, had been unusually gracious. And Bones was unhappy.

There was, in truth, an excellent reason. Bones was one of those uncomfortable people who take a passionate interest in every phase of human activity that happens outside their own especial orbit of duty. He was an officer of Houssas. He enjoyed an allowance from a wealthy uncle, he was living the kind of life he would have chosen of all others, and yet Bones was constantly striving toward perfection in professions which had nothing whatever to do with soldiering. He "took up" almost every branch of study that was offered to him through the advertisement pages of the magazines. He learnt elocution, public speaking, newspaper illustration, short-story writing, motor-car construction, law, motion-picture production, engineering, and the after-care of babies, through the medium of weekly questionnaires and test sheets, though without possessing the slightest aptitude for the practice of a single calling which he so assiduously studied.

And he read. He read the Hundred Best Books and Egyptian History and John Stuart Mill, and books on Inductive and Deductive Logic, and Works of Travel and Sociology. If he did not actually read them, he bought them. Sometimes he read nearly through the first chapter, but generally he read the introduction and put the book away to be read some day "when I can give my mind to it." That day never dawned. Possibly the introductions were sufficient to assure him that they were books he did not wish to know.

Bones was passing through a phase of intellectual development when the inequalities of life were all too apparent. He grieved for his fellowmen. He despised wealth and spoke glibly and contemptuously of capitalism. But for Florence, his life would have been intolerable. Florence was the property of Captain Hamilton. She was a hen, and she was of the Plymouth Rock variety. From her chickhood she had conceived a violent affection for Bones, and Bones, to whom all living things had a soul, had returned her love.

There was an embarrassing side to the friendship, for Florence followed him like a pet dog, and invariably inspected the guard behind him. And the Houssa has a very keen sense of humour.

Yet even Florence did not wholly compensate for the social conditions which were revealed to Bones from week to week in the pages of a fiery periodical which came to him. Bones grew careless in his attire, and addressed Abiboo, his sergeant, as "Comrade." Which Sergeant Abiboo reported to Hamilton.

"It is clear that the young lord Tibbetti has fever," he said, "for this morning he spoke to me as if he were a common man, and said that all men were equal. Even sergeants with privates. Also he said that the land did not belong to Government, but to me and to his lordship. This I report officially."

Finding no traces of fever, Hamilton had given his subordinate three large pills, Bones protesting.

Summoned to the residency, he heard of his projected trip without enthusiasm. Ordinarily the prospect of assuming control of the *Wiggle* would have brought him to a high pitch of ecstasy.

"Thank you, sir an' excellency," he said gloomily. "I'll go because it is my duty. I have a premonition that I may not come back. Instinct, my dear old Ham – I've always been like that. I'm physic."

" 'Psychic' is the word you want," said Hamilton.

"We always call it 'Physic'," said Bones calmly, "and that's the way it's spelt, dear old comrade and OC Troops. If a johnny is physic, surely to good gracious heavens he knows how it's spelt?"

"What have you a premonition of, Bones?" asked Sanders.

Bones made a grimace, lifted his angular shoulders and threw out his hands – gestures indicating his inability to give a plain answer to a plain question.

"Not wishing to cast a dark old shadow or be a jolly old killjoy, I'd rather not say," he replied darkly, "but I've had this feeling, comrade – "

"A little less 'comrade' would be welcome," said Hamilton.

"We're all comrades, dear old officer," said Bones gloomily. "We've got our jolly old social values mixed up. The condition of society with its naughty old artificial restrictions is positively ghastly. It is indeed, old Ham. Sweinmacher says – "

"What Sweinmacher or any other Dutch trader says is immaterial," said Hamilton. "You go to the Isisi this afternoon. And if your premonition comes off I'll write the nicest little obituary notice you've ever seen."

Bones inclined his head gravely. "I've already written it," he said. "You'll find it in my desk, dear old com – officer. You might send it to the *Times* – I've subscribed to that jolly old Thunderer for years, an' they'll be glad to put it in. About 20,000 words as near as I can judge, but if you'd like to add anything to it, I'll take it as a kindness."

Sanders came down to see his subordinate leave.

"N'shimba you will deal with firmly. As yet he is not dangerous. These fellows hold tight to tradition, and until the arrival of the black egg – and the spies say he has been searching for it – there will be no general rising. If necessary, kill N'shimba. You're not taking Florence?"

Florence was perched on the rail of the boat, a brooding, sleepy figure. Undisturbed, she remained when the *Wiggle* cast off and pushed its blunt nose to the rapid waters of the big river.

Bones passed the Isisi country according to plan, and his first call was upon Bosambo, Paramount Chief of the Ochori, and thorn in the side of all kings, chiefs and headmen of the Isisi, Akasava and N'gombi. As well he might be, for he was a Krooman by birth, adventurer by instinct, and a great collector of other men's property by choice.

"I see you one time: I looka you longa longa times, Bonesi. You be good fellow." Thus Bosambo in English, for he had been educated in an English mission school.

Bones struggled hard against resenting the familiarity. Tactfully, he replied in Bomongo.

"Sandi has sent me to speak with your young men, Bosambo, for Sandi's heart is troubled because of this secret society."

"Lord," said Bosambo calmly, "there is no secret society in this land. When the older men join together in dances and call themselves by ghostly names, I say no word, for old men are great talkers and nothing comes of that. But when my young men meet in secrecy, then I know that they will talk scandal. And what is scandalous here in the Ochori but taxation and the punishment I give to evil men? These Young Hearts spoke of me badly, and this I discovered. Now the Young Hearts are not in the Ochori," he added significantly.

Bones considered the matter, scratching his nose. "Bosambo, in this land all men are equal," he said, and the big chief regarded him dispassionately.

"Lord, all men are equal who are equal to one another," he said. "But no man is equal to me, for I am the chief king of the Ochori. And I am not equal to you, Tibbetti, nor you to Sandi. If you are equal to Sandi, speak."

Bones modestly refrained, and the big man went on: "It is right that I should be over the Ochori," he said, "for someone must stand high above the people, or he would not see them well. When there are ten thousand goats upon the plain, what does any goat see but the goat that is next to him? And how may he know what happens on the edge of the flock, where the leopards come crawling and creeping?"

"All men – " began Bones again, but thought better of it. Bosambo was not a man who would be readily convinced.

He secured a certain amount of information about the Young Hearts – information which Bosambo had taken the most drastic measures to procure.

"They are of the Isisi," said Bosambo, "and this king of the Isisi is no man, but a cow. For he sits down and hears these boys speak, and does not beat them. You go to the Isisi, lord?"

Bones went on his way, and his host watched by the riverside, until the white hull of the little *Wiggle* had disappeared round a woody headland. Then Bosambo returned to his hut and to his wife, who was also his counsellor.

"Light of my life," she said in the Arabic of the coast, "Tibbetti has been in many terrible places, but I think the Isisi country will be worse for him."

In two nights and a day Bones came to the Isisi city, and was received in state by the king.

"Lord, I know nothing of the Young Hearts," said Bugulu nervously. "The folly of children is not for me and my wise old men, but for their parents. As to N'shimba, what is he but a child?"

Bones did not attempt to supply an answer to his question. He had not failed to notice, in his walk through the widely scattered city of the king, that, which ever way he looked, he saw no young men. There were those who were old squatting at the fires, and women of all ages going about their proper business. He called the attention of Bugulu to this fact, and the king grew more miserable.

"Lord, they have gone to a palaver in the deep forest," he said. "For these night-talk-people must hold palavers at all times."

Bones hesitated, and then, accompanied by the king, walked down the broad main street of the city. He stopped at the first hut, where an old woman was crushing meal, and spoke to her.

"O woman," he said, "I think you are the mother of sons. Now tell me where your fine son is, that I may speak to him."

She glanced from Bones to the king, and then: "Lord, he is gone to make a palaver in the deep forest," she said.

"What is your son?" asked Bones.

"Master, he is a fisherman and is very stout."

Bones listened to the recital of the young man's virtues, and then asked:

"Bring me his shield and his spear, that I may see them."

The woman looked at the king and at Bones, then turned her eyes away.

"Lord, he has taken his shield and his spear with him, for there is game in the deep forest, and leopards that are terribly fierce," she said.

Apparently, every other young man who had departed out from the Isisi city had also gone in the expectation of meeting terrible leopards.

"These young men say fearful things, Tibbetti," said the old man, troubled. "My own son, who desires to be chief in my place, brought word that you spoke his mind, and that in your heart you were against all chiefs and kings, and the young men believe him. Also that all that is mine is all men's. And that my goats belong to the village and my gardens to every mean man."

"Good gracious heavens alive!" said Bones, aghast, and for the first time there loomed before his eyes a vision of that vast barrier which stands between Utopia and the everyday world.

"Also, lord, they say that men are all as one, as N'shimba the Great also said *cala cala*. And that the young shall rule the world."

"We'll see about that," said Bones, but as he spoke in English the chief thought he was swearing.

Bones went back to the *Wiggle*, and his first act was to cast into the swift black waters of the river a learned treatise on equality by a Russian philosopher who had never met cannibals who believed in ghosts. The book was instantly pouched by a waiting and hungry crocodile, who, perhaps, was best competent to digest it.

Then Bones strapped a Browning to each hip and called Sergeant Ali Ahmed to him.

"Ahmed, I go to make a palaver with the young men of the Isisi."

"Lord comrade – " began the misguided Ahmed, and Bones showed all his teeth.

"If you call me comrade, I will beat the soles of your feet until they are sore," he said. "I want four men who can shoot, and four to carry the little gun that says 'ha-ha.' "

Ahmed saluted and went to parade the men.

An hour's walking along the narrow forest path brought Bones to a clearing where the ground dipped to form an amphitheatre. N'shimba was waiting for him, for news had been brought of his coming. Tail and lank, his body covered with a close-fitting garment of leopard-skin – the wearing of which was a prerogative of chiefs – N'shimba the inspired leant upon his long spear and watched the khaki figure moving slowly toward him.

"I see you, Tibbetti," he called, but did not raise his hand in salute.

"I see you, N'shimba," returned Bones, "and I have come to talk to you, because of certain things which have come to the ears of my lord Sandi. For they say you have a society of Young Hearts."

"They speak true," said N'shimba insolently. "And I, N'shimba N'shamba, am their chief and greater than all chiefs. For I have been called by ghosts and devils to make the Isisi a free people. And I shall be the highest in the land, as the great N'shimba was before me, for his spirit is in my belly."

To his amazement, Bones was neither excited nor showed any visible signs of annoyance.

"That is good talk," said Bones. "Yet those wise men I meet say that the soul of the great N'shimba comes from a black egg. Tell me, man, have you found that egg?"

N'shimba shuffled uneasily. "That will come, Tibbetti, when I have proved my greatness."

"Take me to your Young Hearts," said Bones.

Reluctantly, and with an apprehensive glance at the soldiers, N'shimba led him to the amphitheatre, which now Bones saw for the first time. The slopes of the hollow were black with men, black dappled yellow where the oval shields showed, black which glittered at a thousand points where the sunlight caught the polished heads of the spears. And Bones, without preamble, spoke, and by his side the red-tarboshed soldiers fixed the tripod of the Maxim.

Bones spoke the Bomongo tongue as fluently as a native. He had at his command a range of native imagery which covered all things growing and living. And he talked rapidly and convincingly on the laws of property, and the right of men to eminence. They listened in silence, N'shimba scowling.

When he had finished, they allowed him to go without molestation, Bones in triumph sent a message by pigeon to head-quarters.

"Settled Isisi perlarver. Talked them sily. Knockked ideas out of their joly old crayniums."

Bones had never been strong on spelling.

He had sent the message when Ahmed came to him with news and something in his hand.

"Lord, whilst you made palaver with these boys, the chik–chik sought you in the village, and this came in the very street before the king's house."

Bones looked at the egg in the man's hand and jumped up, his eyes bulging.

It was jet black!

"Moses!" he gasped, and then, in Arabic: "Who saw this?"

"All people, and they were frightened."

"Phew!" said Bones, and turned reproachful eyes upon Florence, who was balancing herself on the back of a chair.

"You're a naughty, naughty girl!" said Bones. "Yes, you are."

Florence made the noise which, in all well-regulated chickens, is the equivalent to a purr.

An hour later came N'shimba.

"Lord," he said respectfully, "there is talk of a wonderful black egg. Now give this to me, and I will be strong for you."

"Man, I am strength itself," said Bones quietly. "As to a black egg, I know of none."

N'shimba went away without protesting further.

At three o'clock, in the dead of the night, the sentry on duty on the *Wiggle* saw a figure crawling stealthily along the deck plank, and shot at it without warning. Bones, running out of his cabin, saw a dead man lying in the light of Sergeant Ahmet's lantern, and the knife clenched between the bared teeth told its own story.

With four men he reached the village. Happily, he had not gone far before the Young Hearts' attack was launched. Fighting his way back to the river, Bones cast off the two steel hawsers as the forerunners of the Young Hearts reached the beach. The *Wiggle* possessed no searchlight, but she carried two Maxim guns, and they sprayed the beach industriously.

In midstream he anchored whilst steam was being raised, and at dawn came a solitary canoe, paddled by a trembling man, who handed up something in a native sack, something that was heavy and wet. Bones guessed the contents before the dead face of the king Bugulu stared up at him.

"Man, who sent this?" he asked the shivering messenger.

"Lord, it was N'shimba," said the man, his teeth chattering. "Also, he spoke to me thus: 'Say to Tibbetti, that I am N'shimba, King of the Isisi and of the Akasava, and of all the peoples of the mountains, and the highest man in all the land. Bring me the black egg and you shall live.'"

Bones did not hesitate. "I go with you," he said, for he knew that the Isisi were night fighters, and that no man would lift spear to him in the open day.

He went ashore. The body of the old king lay stark in the village street, and Bones saw a dead woman lying where she had been speared, and two old men whose age had been an offence.

No man hindered him as he walked slowly to the new king's hut, but the silence was ominous, and, to Bones, menacing.

Before the old king's hut sat N'shimba, the medal of kingship about his neck.

"I see you, white man; give me my pretty egg and you shall live."

Bones took something from his pocket and put it in the new king's hand.

"N'shimba, by magic this thing was born, and it is an egg like none other I have ever seen. Hold it fast, king, and presently your devil shall come out and speak to you, but I must not be here nor any other."

N'shimba nodded gravely. "Let this man go," he said, and Bones walked quickly down the village street.

His foot was in the waiting canoe when he heard the harsh sound of the explosion.

The devil in the black egg had spoken as only a devil can speak when the incautious N'shimba released his grip of the Mills' bomb which Bones had pressed into his hand.

A NICE GEL

Because Terence Doughty was possessed of an immense fortune, was unmarried, and had neither sister nor brother, it was a delicate matter to chide him. At least, so thought his aunts and cousins and other likely beneficiaries of his will.

He was thirty, a little pompous in a reserved way, exceedingly good-looking, and learned to such a terrifying degree that ordinary people cleared their throats before they so much as remarked to him that it was a fine day.

He had written a text-book on Arabic, and he spoke most modern languages. It was a chance reference to the irregular Bomongo verbs, that he read in *Notes and Queries*, that decided him upon taking up the study of native dialects. It happened that there was in London at that time (on sick leave) a missionary from the great river, and from this gentleman Terence learnt, with his usual facility, enough of the language to induce in him a desire for an even further acquaintance.

He announced his scheme to the one aunt who did not stand in awe of the bachelor-millionaire scientist.

"Rubbish!" she snapped. "I've never heard such nonsense! The idea of going into Central Africa to learn verbs! You're either a *poseur* or a fool, Terence. You had much better find a nice gel and settle down in England."

Mr Doughty shuddered. "Gel" always made him shudder.

"My dear aunt! Nice gel!" he mimicked. "I have been looking for that nice gel these ten years! Unfortunately I am cursed with the possession of ideals. These ladies you and the rest of the family have

50

been good enough to choose for me – my God! They are dreadful! There isn't one that doesn't shock all the aestheticism in me."

"What kind of gel do you want?" asked Lady Morestel, curiously.

Lying back in his deep chair, his eyes half closed, his fingertips touching, Mr Terence Doughty enumerated the desirable qualities.

"She must be pretty, of course, that kind of delicate, spiritual prettiness that gives to a woman her most precious mystery. She must be intellectual, yet womanly, in a wistful way. I must be able to love her mind. Refinement of speech and thought, impregnability of ideals – these are amongst the qualities that I seek but do not find."

"You'll not find them in Africa," said her ladyship grimly, and Terence smiled.

"I shall be looking for verbs in Africa," he said. Two months later, Terence Doughty poised himself on the gunwale of the surfboat, his hand upon the bare, brown shoulder of a rower, and, watching his opportunity, jumped almost dry-footed to the yellow sands. One of the crew threw a new suitcase after him.

"Thanks," said Terence.

He was tall and fairly athletic, his face was thin and tanned, his appearance suggested the patronage of a good colonial tailor. Stopping only to light a cigarette, then picking up his grip, he walked toward the residency. Sanders came to meet him.

"Mr Doughty," he said, and Doughty lifted his helmet.

"I'm afraid you hate my coming, sir," he said apologetically.

"I have a bad reputation along the coast," smiled Mr Commissioner Sanders, "and I suppose it is justified. I do not like traders, and I am not, as a rule, enthusiastic about scientific explorers." He walked by the side of the visitor. "What is your itinerary?" he asked.

"I intend going up as far as the Akasava country, then, striking across the French territory to the Congo, follow the river as far as Stanley Falls. After I reach Stanley Falls I shall decide whether I go by rail to Tanganyika and on to Rhodesia, or whether I push across Uganda to the sea. There is one point on which I wanted to speak to you, Mr Sanders, and it is this: I have no timetable, I am moving at my leisure, and it is likely that I shall stop over in certain villages for months at a time. So that if I disappear, I hope I shall not give you any uneasiness."

"You will," said Sanders promptly. "I do not think there is any danger, for the tribes are very quiet just now, but in this land 'to-morrow is a different day,' as the saying goes."

Mr Doughty was introduced to Hamilton of the Houssas, and to Lieutenant Tibbetts, whose other name was Bones, and whilst tiffin was in course of preparation he went down to the quay to examine his heavy baggage that had come on before him, and to try his missionary Bomongo upon the crew of the big canoe which had come down from the Akasava country to take him up river.

"Deuced nice fellow," said Bones thoughtfully. "I've often wished, as you'll bear witness, dear old officer, to make a complete study of these jolly old verbs – what about sending me up with the doughty old Doughty to look after him?"

"I'll say this for you, Bones," said Hamilton, "you're never at a loss to find an excuse for loafing. You stay here and study the jolly old verbs and the payroll and the stores account. And you might give the men a few days' field exercise; they're slacking fearfully."

Bones sighed and abandoned his dream.

So Mr Terence Doughty went alone, and after a month's idling along the river, came in the dark of an evening to a beach.

"We will sleep here tonight," he said, and the headman of the boat grew unexpectedly agitated.

"Lord, we will go on to the city, which we shall reach by the morning. For though my strong paddlers are tired, they will be happy."

"Why not here?" asked Terence in surprise.

The man tapped his teeth with his knuckles. "Lord, this is a magic place. For here is the Tree of the World, and devils live in abundance, so that you cannot walk without treading on their tails. Now let us go on, for my men have fear in their stomachs."

"Land me alone and my little tent," said Terence, now thoroughly interested. "In the morning come for me."

He went ashore on the flat beach and watched the hurried and fearful erection of his tent. They lit a fire for him (all in frantic haste) and paddled away.

Terence had brewed himself a cup of tea and was preparing a meal of canned chicken breast and biscuit, when, raising his eyes suddenly, he saw, standing in the light of the fire, a slim figure. For a second he was startled, and then: "I am M'mina of The Tree," said the girl simply, "and I am a great friend of ghosts."

"O woman, sit with me and eat," said Terence, and she obeyed.

★ ★ ★

There is a tree in the Forest of Happy Dreams, which is in the Akasava country, that has stood from the beginning of time. It is the Tree of the World, and floated in the waters which, according to legend that is so splendidly confirmed by the Jeano-men, was the beginning of all substance. And to the bare roots of the tree came earth, and more earth, and rocks to keep the earth in its place, and mountains to hold the rocks, and so the world was made. It is a cedar of enormous height, which in itself is miraculous, for no other cedars grow in the Akasava. Its branches spread amazingly. Beneath, you may see the rotting stumps of other trees which in the course of hundreds of years have been cut down that the Tree of the World might grow. Some day, so the legend runs, that tree will wither, and on that day the world will begin to go back to the water. First the mountains will crumble and fall into the great river; then the rocks will go to dust, and lastly the earth will dissolve into water and there will be no more earth.

Near by the tree, in a large hut, lived Ogonobo, the Keeper of the Tree, a wise old man, reputedly friend of devils and in the fellowship of ju-jus.

So potent was the mystery of Ogonobo that even M'shimba M'shamba, most ruthless and disrespectful of all great spirits, spared his house on the night of the great wind, when villages and cities were levelled and great gum-trees were plucked up by the roots as though they were corn-stalks.

53

Yet for all his magic and aloofness, Ogonobo was no ascetic. He had taken to himself many wives, and each he had put away because none bore him children. Then he found a fisher girl of no great account and took her into his hut, and she gave him M'mina, a straight-backed, grave-eyed daughter. Some say one thing and some say another about this miracle of a daughter who came to Ogonobo in his old age. Such is the Akasava love for scandal. That his wife had many lovers is true, but what woman of the Akasava is without lovers? Do they not say, "This day I have married a woman who has three husbands" at every wedding feast? Be that as it may, M'mina was a fact, and when old Ogonobo sold his wife to a petty chief this M'mina became the supreme woman of his house, tended his small garden, crushed his corn and cooked for him.

Such men as saw her, hunters who strayed into the ghost forest led by their quarry, feared her. One brought a story that he had seen M'mina sitting on the ground surrounded by thousands of parrots that squawked and chattered to her. And another had seen her in the company of many little birds that came to her when she whistled. It is certain that M'mina was a great charmer of birds, and at her whistle even the fierce hawks stooped and came with a beating of wings to her feet. This was her own peculiar magic.

Incidentally the spirit of the forest came to her, and she communed with devils. One day she came to the old man, her father, and told him.

"Ogonobo," she said, "I saw a little yellow devil sitting under the Tree of the World. He had red eyes, and from his knees grew two hands that pinched me as I passed."

Ogonobo said nothing. He took a long and pliant length of hippo-hide, and he flogged her until he could flog her no more,

"Now, woman," said he, "see no more devils."

M'mina went through the days that followed as though nothing had happened. She slept in a small hut at the back of her father's house, and one night, having a pain in his head, he went to call her that she might boil water for him. She was not on her bed, and, spying, he saw her slip from the forest in the dawn hour and go straight to her hut. He watched her three nights in succession, and every night she went away into the forest and came back with the dawn.

Then he spoke to her. "Woman," he said, "if you have a lover, let him come to me. But if you go in the night to speak to devils, that is bad. For a lover can give you nothing but life, but devils bring trouble. Tell me now, M'mina, which is true?"

"Lord, I go to see devils and one who is greater than all. For he lives in a tree and fire comes from his eyes when he speaks, and one day he will take me into his hut and we shall be happy."

Ogonobo went in search of his thong, and this time the flogging was severe.

"You shall bring no sons of devils into my house, woman," said Ogonobo breathlessly, for he was an old man.

M'mina got up from the floor, rubbing her whealed thighs. Her dark, grave eyes searched the old man's face, and she said: "This night your arm shall die."

"This day my arm is strong," said Ogonobo, and thrashed her again. In this primitive manner did he wage war against the illusions which solitude and a too prolonged austerity might bring to an imaginative mind.

He was sitting before his hut eating his dinner as the sun was setting, and M'mina was crushing corn in a big stone pestle. As the sun touched the trees, the bowl fell from Ogonobo's hand, and when he tried to pick it up his right arm refused to obey. From shoulder to fingertip he was paralysed.

"Woman, come here," he said, and the girl obeyed, standing before him, silent and watchful.

"My arm is dead, as you promised. Now I see that you are a great witch, and I am afraid. Touch my arm and make it well."

As she bent down to perform this service, his well hand shot out, and he caught her swiftly by the throat and threw her backward over his knees.

"It is better that I have one arm than none," he said, "or no arms than that I be dead. I am too old to live in fear of death; therefore, M'mina, my daughter, you go quickly to the Place of Ghosts."

She lay unstruggling as the pressure of his sinewy fingers increased, and when it seemed to him that she was resigned to death, with a strength that he had not guessed, she flung herself free from him and fled into the hut. He rose a little awkwardly and followed. As he stooped to enter the low door, she struck at him twice with the long-handled N'gombi axe that he kept to trim away the tree. Ogonobo coughed thickly and went down on to his knees, clutching with his one hand at the doorway's edge.

"Death," said M'mina, and brought the keen edge to his unprotected neck with all her power...

When she had buried him and had cleaned away the mess, she went back to her corn, and, carrying the pestle into the hut, lay down on her bed and slept. And she sat in Ogonobo's place and said magic words to the tree, and held communion with ghosts of all colours.

One day she went on a journey into the city of the king and stood before his house, and Ofaba, the king, who had heard of her, came out.

"I see you, M'mina, daughter of Ogonobo, the Keeper of the Tree. Where is your father?"

"Lord, he is dead, and his mystery is mine. And I sit in the Forest of Dreams and many pleasant devils make love to me. One I shall marry soon, and on that night M'shimba M'shamba shall come to my hut and sing my marriage song."

Ofaba shivered and spat. "How did Ogonobo die, woman?" he asked. "One of my young men when hunting saw blood on the leaves."

"A devil killed him with a great axe that was bigger than the Tree of the World. And I fought with the devil by my magic, and he is dead too. And I cut him into pieces, and one of his legs I threw into the Little River, and it overflowed, as all men know."

That the Little River had overflown Ofaba knew. The rains had been heavy, but the Little River had never overflown before. Here, then, was an explanation more in harmony with Ofaba's known predilection for the mysterious and the magical.

"This I came to tell you, lord," she said. "Also that I had a dream, and in this dream I saw Bosambo of the Ochori, who was on his knees before you, Ofaba, and you put your foot on his neck, and said 'Wa,' and Bosambo shook with fear."

Ofaba himself trembled with something that was not fear, for she had dreamt his dream. This he did not tell her, sending her away with presents, and by certain wonderful acts confirming her in her office.

It is a saying in the Akasava country, that the child of the eaten moon is a great glutton, and Ofaba M'lama, the son of B'suri, King of the Akasava and paramount lord of the Ten Little Rivers, was so born. For the moon was at its last quarter when he came squealing into the world, and B'suri, looking up at the fading crescent, said, having a grievance: "This child will eat. Let him eat the Ochori."

A wise saying, so frequently repeated to Ofaba, long after he had taken B'suri's stool of office and his great silver medal of chieftainship; long after B'suri had been paddled stark to the middle island where dead men lie in shallow graves.

Ofaba needed little to remind him that the Akasava hated the Ochori, because that was traditional. *Cala cala*, which means "Years ago," the Ochori had been the slave tribe, a debased and fearful people who, at the first hint of danger, ran away into the woods with their wives and children and such goats as they could grab. Sometimes they left their wives behind, but there is no record of their having gone entirely goatless.

So it was that, what any nation needed, they took from the Ochori, and if the taking was bloodless, no strong word went down to the ear of Mr Commissioner Sanders, who sat between sea and river in a large thatched house and gave judgment impartially. But there came to the Ochori a certain man from the Kroo Coast, an escaped convict, one Bosambo, who, by the employment of questionable methods, had secured his election to the kingship. And with his coming there had arisen a new spirit in the Ochori, so that when the Akasava or the Isisi raided their lands, they were met by locked shields and a phalanx of spears, and there was a killing or two.

Ofaba was now a man of twenty-three, and in the year when M'mina became the Keeper of the Tree, the harvests of the Akasava failed, for no especial or understandable reason. Ofaba and his wise men gathered in secret council, and in the dark hours of the night they took from his bed a youth who was silly with sleeping sickness, and, carrying him into the woods, they cut his throat with the razor edge of Ofaba's hunting spear, and sprinkled his blood on that old and sacred tree which had stood from the beginning of time.

M'mina watched the ceremony from the door of her hut, and when it was over came forth.

"I see you, Ofaba, also this man whom you have killed because your crops have failed. Now, I have talked with my husband, who comes to me every night in the shape of a bat, and he says that the crops have failed because of Bosambo, the chief man of the Ochori. That day you bring him to me, that day shall the crops grow and the game come back to the forest. For I will make a great magic with Bosambo that will be wonderful to see. You shall make an end to Bosambo, as I have made to his spies. Come."

Bewildered, the king followed her through the dark forest and came to the beach. Here, hidden by bushes, were three graves.

"O woman!" he gasped. "What evil have you done? For if Sandi knows — "

"Shall Sandi know the blooding of the tree?" she asked significantly, and Ofaba sweated. "Now, I tell you that when Bosambo himself comes, as he will, you shall bring him here. And you shall be happy."

*　★　★*

At headquarters, Mr Commissioner Sanders was in a peculiarly complacent frame of mind. For two months there had been no sign or sound of trouble in his territory. Mr Terence Doughty, that fastidious grammarian, had passed to the French territory (Bosambo had sent a long message by pigeon post announcing his passage); the crops, with the exception of the Akasava mealie crop, had been good. Taxation was being voluntarily liquidated.

"In fact, everything is almost too good to be true," he said one evening as they sat in the cool of the verandah.

That night he was wakened from a sound sleep by a hullaballoo that brought him to the open, revolver in hand. A knot of men were struggling noisily somewhere in the darkness, and Hamilton, who joined him, offered an explanation.

"One of my infernal Houssas," he swore. "Where these devils get gin from, heaven knows – Bones!"

Bones answered from the darkness. "Naughty old thief trying to get into the residency, Ham, old thing – "

Five minutes later a dishevelled Bones in pyjamas and mosquito boots came to report.

"Chucked him in the guard-room," he said. "By gad, if I hadn't seen him you might have been robbed, dear old excellency – murdered, dear old Ham. If this isn't worth a special report and a DSO, then there's no justice on this wicked old earth."

"Did you spot him?" asked Hamilton incredulously.

"I didn't exactly spot him, sir and brother officer," said Bones with care. "In theory I did, old captain. Ahmet saw him sneaking across the square, and of course I was on the spot in two shakes of a duck's jolly old rudder."

Sergeant Ahmet supplemented the information. He had seen the marauder and had leapt at him.

"When we wakened my lord Tibbetti, he ordered the bad man to prison."

"What do you mean – 'wakened'?" demanded Bones indignantly. "O Ahmet, was I not there – did I not – ?"

"Why ask this unfortunate man to perjure himself?" demanded Hamilton. "Go back to bed, Phyllis; you're losing your beauty sleep."

The buglers were sounding reveille, and the brown-legged guard stood rigidly before the guardhouse, their rifles at the slope, their expressionless brown faces strained and intense, looking at nothingness.

Lieutenant Tibbetts, in khaki, a long sword slapping at his leg, stalked over from his hut, his helmet tilted over one eye in the fashion set by a remarkable admiral, and coming to a halt before the guard, glared at the four inoffensive soldiers.

"The guard is present, lord," said the sergeant in his queer, guttural Arabic.

"Let it be dismissed, Ahmet," said Bones. "Now bring me the prisoner."

There came, blinking into the light from the dark prison hut, a man, at the sight of whom Lieutenant Tibbetts' jaw dropped – and it took a lot (as Bones often said) to surprise him.

"Bosambo!" he squeaked in English. "Goodness gracious heavens alive, well I'm dashed!"

The big man grinned sheepishly. "I be damned, sah, too, one time. I make 'um foolish all time, Bonesi."

"Not so much of that Bonesi," said Bones severely. "You naughty old reveller – you disgustin' carousin' old sinner. Really, really, Bosambo, I wonder you're not ashamed of yourself!"

Bosambo did not look particularly ashamed, although he, king and paramount chief of the Ochori, had suffered the indignity of spending a night in the guard-room, and had been carried there in the middle of the night by four stalwart Houssas.

"I no be drunken, Tibbetti," he began earnestly. "I be good Matt'ew Marki Luki Christian – "

"Monkey talk," said Bones unpleasantly, and this time he spoke in Bomongo.

"Lord," said Bosambo in that language, "I came by night because of certain news which my spies brought to me. And because I came secretly, not wishing your lordship's soldiers to know me, I did not tell them who I was when they fell upon me as I crossed the square. And if I fought them, using terrible words, there was this reason, for I thought that in the night I could break away from the little prison and go my way."

Bones went up to the residency, leaving the "prisoner" in his own hut. Hamilton, shaving (in his pyjamas) on the verandah, saw the martial figure – he would have heard the slap of the sword anyway – and suspended operations.

"Morning, Mars – is there a war on?" he demanded, returning to his grimaces at the mirror and the manipulation of his safety razor.

"Dear old officer, there are certain aspects of military service that no self-respecting old commander jests about," said Bones testily. "If I hadn't turned out in jolly old regimentals, you would have kicked."

"Well, did you court-martial and shoot the noisy devil?" asked Hamilton. "He woke Sanders – who was he and what was he doing? Abiboo said it was somebody trying to break into the residency."

"It was Bosambo," said Bones, with dramatic emphasis.

He was entitled to enjoy the sensation his words created.

"Bo – sambo? Bosh!"

Bones raised his eyebrows and closed his eyes. "Very good, jolly old sir. I have done my duty: I can do no more," he said.

"Bosambo!"

Sanders stood in the doorway, and Bones saluted.

"Yes, excellency: Bosambo. I had a suspicion it was he last night."

"You said that you knew it was a Lower River fisherman who had got square face," began Hamilton, but Sanders' hand called for silence.

"Send him here, Bones," he said quietly.

Bosambo arrived, more self-possessed than Bones thought was decent.

"Lord, it is true that it was I who came like a thief, desiring secret word with you," he said frankly, "for this is a big thing that I had to tell, and my stomach was troubled."

"You have brought me much news before," said Sanders sternly, "yet you came in daylight and met me in palaver. Now you come like an Isisi robber, and my soldiers have shamed you, and therefore have shamed me and my king. Are there no grey birds or swift messengers?"

"Lord, there are all these," said Bosambo calmly. "One grey pigeon came to me last week, and about his little red leg was a book* which

---

* Letter.

said that I must not seek Dhoti any more, as he had gone a long journey into the Lower Isisi."

Sanders sat up in his chair with a start. "Man, what are you saying? I sent no message but about your taxation."

Bosambo fumbled in his leopard-skin robe and took out a folded paper, handing it to the Commissioner without a word.

Sanders read and frowned. "I did not send this message," he said. "As to Dhoti,* he went into the Frenchi country two moons gone, and you sent me a book saying this."

"Lord," said Bosambo, "I sent no such book, nor have I seen Dhoti. And because of things I heard, I sent my spies into the Akasava and they did not come back. I myself would have gone, but my young and cunning listeners told me that Ofaba waited to seize me, and his canoes watched the river. So, lord, I came secretly."

Sanders fingered his chin, his face set and hard.

"Get steam in the *Zaire*, Hamilton. I leave for the Upper River just as soon as you are ready. I shall want ten soldiers and a rope."

★ ★ ★

In the deepest jungle of the Forest of Dreams, and in a secret place between two marshes was a hut, and stretched on a bed of skins before the door lay a young man. He was yellow of face, unshaven, gaunt. The fever which comes to white men in this forest of illusions was on him, and his teeth chattered dismally. Nevertheless, he smiled, and his eyes lit up as the girl came from a belt of trees, carrying in her arms a large and steaming pot.

"By jove, M'mina, I am glad to see you," he said in English, as he reached out and took her hand.

"My husband and my lover," she murmured, fondling the thin fingers between her palms, "I do not understand you when you speak with that tongue. I have brought you food, and I have spoken with the devils that you shall get well."

* Doughty.

Terence chuckled weakly. "The grey birds have not come?" he asked.

"One will come soon – my spirit tells me," she said, squatting on the ground by the side of him.

He dropped his arm on her shoulder and looked fondly down into the round and comely face.

"There is no woman like you in the world, M'mina. You are the most wonderful of all. And I will take you across the black water, and you shall be a great lady."

"Lord, I will stay here, and you also," she said calmly; "for I knew when I saw you first, that you were the husband that the ghosts had whispered to me about."

He was looking at her raptly. "O woman," he said in Bomongo, "you are very beautiful." And then he stopped, for her eyes were searching the heavens. Suddenly she sprang up, and, pursing her lips, sent forth a long trill of melody. It was less a whistle than a high vocal note, and though it was not loud, the swift bird that was crossing the patch of sky checked, wheeled and came in narrowing circles lower and lower, till it dropped at her feet. She stooped, picked up the grey pigeon and smoothed its plumage. Then, with fingers deft with practice, she took the tissue paper that was fastened about the leg by a rubber band and gave it to the man.

He peered down at the Arabic characters. "It is from Sandi to Bosambo," he said, "and he says all is well."

She nodded. "Then this little bird may go," she answered; "and my lord need not write any message to deceive the fat man of the Ochori. Lord, I fear this man, and have spoken with Ofaba that he may be killed."

Terence Doughty fell back on his pillow and closed his eyes.

"You're a wonderful girl," he murmured in English, and she tried to repeat the words. "Clever girl...what a splendid mind you must have!"

She stooped and covered him with a skin rug, and then, at the sound of footsteps, she turned quickly. A lean man in white duck was crossing the clearing, and behind him she saw the glint of steel and the red tarbosh of soldiers.

"O Sandi," she greeted him without embarrassment, "so you have found me and my husband."

"And three little graves, M'mina," said Sanders quietly. "Now you shall answer to me for your life."

She shook her head. "You will not kill me, Sandi, because that is not your way. In all time you have never hanged any woman from the high tree, and I think I shall live, because I am well loved by certain devils and ghosts, and my ju-ju is strong for me. Also for this man."

Terence was staring up at Sanders, a frown on his emaciated face.

" 'Morning," he said, a little resentfully. "You know my wife?"

"I know her very well," said Sanders softly.

"Hope you didn't mind my fooling round with your messages," said Doughty. "By the way, I've at last got the Bomongo word for…"

His voice sank into a drowsy murmur. Mr Terence Doughty did not wholly recover consciousness until he was halfway on the voyage to England, and then he woke as from a bad dream. In that dream there figured a strange and gracious figure, which he could not identify or remember. All his life, even when he was comfortably and respectably married, there hovered in the background of his mind the illusion of a greater happiness which he had once experienced.

Sitting in the Village of Irons, in that portion reserved for the women who had worked evilly against the Government, M'mina often said to her fellows in durance: "Sandi has taken my man, but my soul and spirit and ghost is with him always, and my devil shall whisper in his ear: 'M'mina waits for you in the Forest of Dreams.' "

Which in a sense was a perfectly true statement, though Terence Doughty would have been shocked if he could have identified the woman who flitted through his thoughts and was the foundation of many dreams…

Once he woke with a cry, and his wife asked him if he was ill.

"No, no… I was thinking…a nice gel… I wonder who she was?"

His wife smiled. She was wise enough never to probe into the past, but sometimes she wondered who that nice gel was.

THE BRASS BEDSTEAD

There is no tribe on the river that has not its most secret mystery. In the course of the years, Mr Commissioner Sanders had acquired a working knowledge of hundreds, yet was well aware that he had but touched the fringe of multitudes. For within every mystery is yet another. He knew that within the pods of a specie of wild pea there dwelt a beneficent spirit called "Cha", that brought luck and prosperity, but that if the pea was split into four and given to four people, one would die within a moon, but he did not learn for years that if one of the four quarters remained green, there would be no fish in the river for the space of nine moons.

Every plant and flowering tree had its peculiar familiar, good or bad, and once he had been brought a hundred and fifty miles to a great palaver, and all because a mealy stalk had produced only one cob – which was a sign of coming pestilence. Sometimes a peculiar potent would not appear at all and a hundred thousand men and women would sit and shiver their apprehension, whilst search parties would go forth and seek it.

In the end Sanders evolved a formula. At headquarters was a squat concrete house, built at the time of a serious war to store ammunition. The magazine was still employed for that purpose, but Sanders found it a new use. It became a repository of ju-jus. When M'shimba M'shamba (which is another name for a small typhoon) did not put in an appearance, and the Isisi and N'gombi people met in solemn conclave to discuss what evil had been done that the great green spirit did not walk abroad, Sanders came.

"Have no fear, for M'shimba stays with me in my Ghost House, being very weary."

When the famous Tree of the World was uprooted in a storm and swept out of sight down the river, Sanders could reassure a trembling people.

"This great tree Is. It lives in my strange House of Ghosts, and none other shall see it. There it sits making good magic for the Isisi."

Bones came to be custodian of the Ghost House by natural processes. Finding that certain credit attached to the position, he claimed it for his own, and when the lower river folk lost their ju-ju (maliciously conveyed on to the *Zaire* by a native workman and concealed in the engine furnace) Bones assumed responsibility.

"This fine ju-ju came to my Ghost House, and there he lives, and every morning I speak to him and he speaks to me."

"Lord, we should like to see our beautiful ju-ju, for he was made wonderfully out of a magic tree by our fathers," said one of the troubled elders.

"Him you may see," said Bones significantly, "but if you look upon the other ghosts who live with him, your eyes will fall out."

They decided to leave the ju-ju to his tender care.

The plan worked exceedingly well until Bosambo fell out with the Akasava.

Bosambo, Paramount Chief of the Ochori, best-eared of all chiefs, had an elementary but effective system of justice. For him no frontiers existed, no sovereignty was sacred, though he rigidly enforced the restrictions of frontier and the holiness of the Ochori territory upon others. There came into the forest land at the extreme southern edge of his land a party of Akasava huntsmen in search of game, and these with a lordly indifference to the inviolability of his territory, speared and shot without so much as "by your leave."

They were in search of the small monkeys with white whiskers, which are considered a delicacy by the epicureans of the Akasava, and are found nowhere else than in the southern Ochori. They are killed with arrows, to the heads of which a yard of native rope is attached. When the monkey is hit, the barbed arrowhead falls off, and the rope and shaft becoming entangled in the small branches of the trees in which the little people live, they are easily caught and despatched.

Now the people of the Ochori do not eat monkeys. They capture them and train them into domestic pets, so that you cannot pass through an Ochori village without seeing little white-whiskered figures squatting contentedly on the roof of the huts, engaged mainly in an everlasting hunt for fleas.

Messengers brought news of the invasion, and Bosambo left hurriedly for the south, taking with him fifty spearmen. They came upon the Akasava hunting party sitting about a fire over which shrivelled monkey-meat was roasting.

What followed need not be described in these pure pages; Bosambo had no right to brand the poachers with red-hot spear blades, and certainly his treatment did not err on the side of delicacy.

Ten days later, the weary hunting party came to the Akasava city and carried their grievances.

"Lord king, this Bosambo beat us and put hot irons upon us, so that we must sleep on our faces and cannot sit because of the cruel pain. And when we spoke of our king, he made horrible faces."

Here was a cause for war, but the crops were not in, so the king sent his eldest men to Sanders. There was a palaver, and Sandi gave judgment.

"If a man walks into the lair of a leopard, shall he come to me and say, 'I am scratched'? For the leopards have their place, and the hunter has his. And if a man put his hand into a cooking-pot, shall he kill the woman at the fire because his hand is burnt? There is a place for the hand and a place for the boiling meat. Now, I give you this riddle. How can a man be burnt if he does not go to the fire? Let no man of the Akasava hunt in the forests of the Ochori. As to the lord chief Bosambo, I will make a palaver with him."

"Lord," said one of the injured hunters, "we are shamed before our wives, and we cannot sit down."

"Stand," said Sanders laconically; "and as to your wives, this is a wise saying of the Akasava: 'No man turns his face to the sun or his back to his wife.' The palaver is finished."

He saw Bosambo in the privacy of his hut, and the interview was brief.

"Bosambo, you shall neither maim nor kill, nor shall you put other people to shame. If these men hunt in your forest, do you not fish in their waters? They tell me, too, that you take your spears to the Akasava country and clear their woods of meat. This is my word, that you shall not again go into their hunting-grounds, until they come to yours."

"Oh ko!" said Bosambo in dismay; for the taboo which had been put upon him was the last he desired.

Bosambo had an affection for a kind of wild duck that could only be trapped in the Akasava marshes, and the deprivation was a serious one.

"Lord," he said, "I have repented in my heart, being a Christian, the same as you, and being well acquainted with Marki, Luki and Johnny, and other English lords. Let the Akasava come to my forest, and I will go to their lands to catch little birds. For, lord, I did not hurt these Akasava men, merely burning them in play, thinking they would laugh."

Sanders did not smile. "Men do not laugh when they are so burnt," he said, and refused to lift the embargo.

"If they come to you, you may go to them," he said at parting.

For the greater part of three months Bosambo was Tempter. He withdrew his spies from the forest, he sent secret word to the Akasava king, inviting him to great hunts; he conveyed taunts and threats calculated to arouse all that was warlike in his bosom, but the Akasava king rejected the overtures and returned insult for insult. And Bosambo brooded on roast duck and grew morose.

Then on a day Sanders had a message from one of his spies who kept a watchful eye upon the people of the Akasava. And there was need for watchfulness, apart from the trouble with Bosambo, for it had been a year of record crops, and when the crops are plentiful and goats multiply in the Akasava country, and men grow rich in a season, and are relieved for the moment of the strain which judiciously applied taxation and the stubbornness of the soil impose, their minds turn to spears, and to the ancient stories of Akasava valour which the old men tell and the young maidens sing. And they are apt, in their pride, to look around for new enemies, or to furbish old grievances. For this is the way of all peoples, primitive or civilised, that prosperity and idleness are the foundations of all mischief.

Cala cala, which means long ago, the N'gombi people, who were wonderful workers of iron, had stolen a bedstead of solid brass, bequeathed to the king of the Akasava by a misguided missionary, who in turn had received it from as misguided a patron. And this bedstead of brass was an object of veneration and awe for twenty years; and then, in a little war which raged for the space of three moons between the Akasava and the N'gombi, the Akasava city had been taken and sacked, and the bed of brass had gone across the river into the depths of the forest, and there, by cunning N'gombi hands, had reappeared in the shape of bowls and rings and fine-drawn wire of fabulous value. For any object of metal is an irresistible attraction to the craftsmen of the forest — did not Sanders himself lose a steel anvil from the lower deck of the *Zaire?* The story of how ten men swam across the river, carrying that weight of metal, is a legend of N'gombi.

The true city of these people is situated two days' march in the forest; and hither, one fine morning, came messengers from the king of the Akasava — four haughty men, wearing feathers in their hair and leopard skins about their middle, and each man carrying a new shield and a bunch of bright killing spears, which the N'gombi eyed with professional interest.

"O king, I see you," said the chief envoy, one M'guru. "I am from your master, the king and lord of the Akasava, who, as you know, are the greatest people in these lands, being feared even by Sandi because of their valour and wonderful courage."

"I have heard of such people," said the king of the N'gombi, "though I have never seen them, except the spearers of fish who live by the riverside."

This was designed and accepted as a deadly insult, for the Akasava are great fish-eaters, and the N'gombi do not eat fish at all, preferring frogs and snakes (as the slander goes).

"My king will bring his people to see you," said the envoy significantly. "And this he will do soon, if you do not return to us the bedstead you stole *cala cala*, and which my king desires."

The king of the N'gombi was smoking a long-stemmed pipe with a tiny bowl, and the rancid scent of the native tobacco was an offence to the nose of the Akasava messenger.

"Am I M'shimba M'shamba, that I can bring from nothing something?" he asked. "As to your bedstead, it is not! Nor will it ever be again. Take this word to the little king of the Akasava, that I am M'shulu-M'shulu, son of B'faro, son of M'labo, son of E'goro, who put the Akasava city to the flames and carried away the bedstead which was his by right. That I, this man who speaks, will meet the Akasava, and many will run quickly home, and they will run with the happiest, for they will be alive. This palaver is finished."

All this the embassy carried back to the Akasava, and the *lokalis* beat, the young men danced joyously, as young men will when the madness of war comes to a people: and then, when secret preparations had been completed, and all was in readiness, an Akasava man, walking through the forest by the river, saw a foreigner throw a pigeon into the air, and the man was brought to the king of the Akasava, and a council of war was held. The prisoner was brought, bound, before the king.

"O man," said he, "you are a spy of Sandi's, and I think you have been speaking evilly of my people. Therefore you must die."

The Kano boy accepted the sentence philosophically. "Lord king," he said, "I have a great ju-ju in a little basket. Let me speak to him before I die, and I will speak well of you to the ghosts of the mountains."

They brought him the basket and the pigeon it contained, and he fondled it for five minutes, and none saw him slip into the red band about the pigeon's leg a scrap of paper no larger than a man's thumb. Then, before they could realise what was happening, the pigeon had been flung into the air and was flying, with long, steady strokes and ever widening circles, higher and higher, until it was beyond the reach of the arrows that the young men shot.

Six young warriors carried Ali, the Kano boy, into the forest. Bending down a young sapling, they fastened a rope to the top, the other end fastened in a noose about the spy's neck. His feet were pinioned to the ground, so that he was stretched almost to choking by the upward tug of the tree. The king himself struck off the head with a curved N'gombi knife, and that was the end of Ali the spy.

Three days passed in a final preparation, and on the morning of the fourth the king of the Akasava assembled his fighting men by the riverside; their war-painted canoes blackened the beach, their spears glittered beautifully in the sun.

"O people," said the king, exalted to madness, "we go now to make an end of the N'gombi..."

His speech was nearing its peroration – for he was a notorious talker – when the white nose of the *Zaire* came round the wooded headland that hides the course of the river from sight.

"This is real war," said the king, and hardly had he spoken before a white puff of smoke came from the little steamer; there was a whine, a crashing explosion, and all that remained of the haughty king of the Akasava was an ugly mess upon the beach – it was a most fortunate shot.

Sanders came ashore with fifty Houssas and four machine-guns; there was no resistance, and Kofaba, the king's nephew, reigned in his place.

At the Palaver of All People, Sanders disposed, as he hoped, for ever of the brass bedstead.

"This brass bedstead lives for all time in my ghost house, with ju-jus and other wonderful things, for *cala cala* I took it from N'gombi by magic and put it away that there should be no more wars. And Tibbetti, who is the Keeper of the House, sees this every morning and every night and touches it lovingly. Because it is the property of the Akasava and like no other in the world, I keep it, and no other nation, neither the N'gombi nor the Isisi, nor the little bushmen nor the Ochori, shall see this great treasure."

The vigilant Bosambo, who had gathered his fighting regiments in readiness to intervene, dismissed them in disgust when he learnt of the

71

comparatively peaceful termination of the dispute. Bosambo had visions of new treaties and the removal of old restrictions, and it was a disappointment to him to learn that the dispute had ended so bloodlessly.

The cause of the quarrel was plain to him, and for some time made no impression, for ghosts and ju-jus and occult mysteries of all kinds had no place in his practical system. He began fresh negotiations with the new king of the Akasava, and sent two of his councillors on an embassy of congratulation, accompanied by a large bag of salt as a peace offering.

But Kofaba was no more amenable than had been his uncle.

"Go back to Bosambo, the little chief," he said, with the arrogance of his new dignity upon him, "and tell him that I, Kofaba, am Sandi's man and will keep Saudi's law. As to the salt, it is bad salt, for it has fallen into the water and is hard."

This was perfectly true. Bosambo, who was of an economical mind, kept that salt bag as a permanent offering. It was the custom of chiefs and kings to greet one another with presents, though the ceremony was more or less perfunctory, and the present was invariably returned with polite expressions of gratitude.

It is true that Bosambo had returned nothing; that he kept the bag of damaged salt in case some dignitary of the land, who hadn't sufficient decency to return his proffered gift, should accept the salt.

Bosambo received the message wrathfully. "It seems that this Kofaba is a common man," he said. "Now sit with me in palaver, and we will think great thoughts."

The palaver lasted for the greater part of four days, and every plan for the invasion of his kingdom was rejected. Bosambo might have sent forth his own poachers to satisfy his gastronomical needs, but he was a queer mixture of lawlessness and obedience to law, and would no more have thought of breaking his word to Sandi than he would of murdering his wife.

Then, on the fourth day, a great thought came to his mind. In the evening he sent a canoe with six paddlers to the mouth of the river, for he remembered that it was the time of the year when Halli, the trader, came to the river.

On a certain day, following the despatch of his mission, a crazy old tub, that had the appearance of a barge which had seen better days, came slowly along the coast, keeping close to the beach, for its skipper was taking no chances.

Barge or lighter it had been. The stern wheel, that creaked as it turned, was obviously homemade and home-fitted. The engine-house was no more than a canopy of rusty galvanised iron, through which poked the black snout of something that had once been a donkey engine, and was now the chief motive power of the *Comet* – such was the name of this strange craft.

Amidships were three thatched huts, the sleeping apartments of the officers in command. Before these stretched an awning which covered a raised platform, on which a man in a battered and dingy white helmet manipulated the steering wheel.

By a miracle the *Comet* rounded the point and came slowly up the river. Opposite the residency quay the captain struck a big brass gong twice, and four perspiring natives cast an anchor overboard. The gong sounded three times, and the engines stopped.

Passing back to examine the steam gauge, the captain washed his hands, lighted a long, thin cigar, and, stepping into the canoe that had been dropped for him, he was paddled ashore.

He was tall and lean, and his face was the colour of Egyptian pottery. His age was somewhere between twenty-five and thirty-five.

Bones stood on the quay watching the arrival of the craft. The manoeuvring of the *Comet* was to him a subject of fascinating interest.

"Good Halley; the jolly old ship's still floating?"

"Yes, she's still floating," agreed the other gravely.

He was slow of speech, being unused to English, which he spoke very seldom, though it was his native tongue.

"Is Mr Sanders at headquarters? I want permission to trade up as far as Lobosolo on the Isisi, and I'm taking up some stuff to Bosambo."

"What's your deadly cargo?" asked Bones.

"Whisky and machine-guns, *as* usual," said the other more gravely. "We are thinking of introducing cocaine and mechanical pianos next voyage."

Halley and Halley's *Comet* were known from Ducca to Mossamedes. He was a one-man trader who from time to time dared the dangers of the deep for his immediate and personal profit. In this crazy ship of his he penetrated rivers, explored strange streams, exchanging his beads and looking-glasses for rubber and ivory and the less valuable products that native industry produces. He was invariably fair in his dealings, and had a reputation for honesty that carried over a million square miles of country.

Sanders welcomed him with a geniality which he offered to few other traders. He knew that there were no cheap German rifles concealed at the bottom of the *Comet's* cargo, nor illicit bottles of synthetic gin artfully hidden beneath bolts of Manchester goods. Halley was white in every sense, and whitest in his dealing with the women of the backlands.

"The country is quiet and the people are fairly happy," he said. "Avoid the Tugesini River – there is another outbreak of smallpox there…the N'gombi have been trapping leopards, and you should get some good skins."

They gossiped of the people, of their idiosyncrasies and peculiar tastes. Of how the Akasava never bought mirrors, and the queer passion of the Lesser Isisi folk for aluminium saucepans.

That afternoon, the *Comet* went on its slow way, its donkey engine puffing noisily.

"Queer bird," said Hamilton, watching the departing boat. "I wonder what the dickens he is doing with Ochori paddlers – did you notice them, sir?"

Sanders nodded. "Bosambo sent them up the coast a month ago – he's a great shopper. I wonder what stuff Halley is taking to our friend. I meant to ask him."

Bosambo was the one chief of the territory who held any communication with the outside world. He waited patiently for the arrival of the *Comet*, and when the ship came wallowing round the green bluff that hid the lower reaches of the river, Bosambo went down in state to meet his visitor, and for three days there were great bargainings and hagglings, Bosambo squatting on the untidy deck, Halley in his skin-seated chair.

"Effendi," said Bosambo (it was his title of honour for all strangers), "for all I buy I will pay in white man's money."

Halley was gratified, but sceptical, and when Bosambo produced bags of shining coin, he was agreeably surprised. If he tried samples of the first bag in his strong white teeth, he did not test the second bag at all.

Halley brought his eccentric boat to the mouth of the river, in the dark hours of the morning, and Bones, going down to the beach for his dip, saw the *Comet* crawling along the coast, no unusual circumstance, for the trader never stopped at the residency on his homeward voyage unless a sea was running. As it happened, Mr Halley had nothing to stop for, since there had been no unusual happening to report.

★ ★ ★

"Have you ever thought, dear old sir, what a dinky little ice plant you could rig up in that old dug-out?" asked Bones, standing, his arms akimbo, before the grey door of the magazine. "A refrigeratin' plant, dear old Ham – we might even get some skatin'!"

"I've often thought I'd like to see it a little cleaner than it is," said Hamilton. "Have it turned out and lime-washed, Bones – and for heaven's sake let the men do the whitewashing."

"My dear old officer," said Bones reproachfully, "as if I should turn myself into a jolly old paperhanger an' decorator!"

Nevertheless he came to lunch next day with boots that were splashed white and a long streak of whitewash on his nose.

"By the way, have you a great deal of ammunition in stock, Hamilton?" asked Sanders, who had been very quiet through lunch.

"The regulation amount, sir," said Hamilton in surprise. "A thousand rounds per man – why, are you expecting trouble?"

"No," said Sanders shortly, and Hamilton knew from his brusque tones that the Commissioner's uncanny instinct was at work.

"Maybe dear old excellency is worryin' about my gettin' a splash of whitewash in my eye," suggested Bones.

"Maybe he isn't," replied Hamilton.

"It's a funny thing about me, dear old Ham — " began Bones, but his superior was not in the mood to discuss the many funny aspects of Bones which had struck him from time to time. For Sanders' anxiety had communicated itself to him. And yet there was no apparent reason for uneasiness; by the reports that came to headquarters, peace and prosperity were the orders of the day from one end of the river to the other.

But Hamilton knew, as Sanders knew, that this condition of affairs was the invariable preliminary to all outbreaks and disturbances. The bolts, the real bolts, fell from a cloudless sky. Secretly Sanders preferred a condition when little quarrels between the tribes completely occupied their minds. Native people cannot think of two things at once. They are children who live in and for the day. Yesterday is *cala cala*, tomorrow is the dim and misty future.

And then, one sleepy afternoon...

By all the laws of average and chance, Bones should have been killed. As it was, he sneezed, and when Bones sneezed, his body fell into strange and fearful contortions. Sometimes he sneezed forward and finished up with his head between his knees (you must suppose him sitting in the shade of his verandah); sometimes he sneezed backward and his head jerked over the rail of his deck-chair, and, to the alarmed spectator, seemed in danger of dropping off. Usually he sneezed forward, but this time he raised his contorted visage to the heavens and sneezed at the blue skies. And the arrow, missing his throat, struck a pole of the verandah and stuck quiveringly.

Lieutenant Tibbetts looked at the deadly shaft, dazed for a second. Then he rose quickly and went into his hut. He was out again in a second, a sporting Lee Metford in his hand. A glance at the arrow showed the direction. It had come from a clump of cotton bush at the far side of the parade ground, and, sinking to one knee, Bones aimed at the ground-line and fired.

The "pang!" of the shot brought the Houssa guard tumbling out of their hut, but before the sergeant could reach him, the long legs of Bones were flying across the parade in the direction of the bushes. He heard a shout, and out of the corner of his eye he saw Hamilton leap the verandah and pelt along after him, but he did not slacken his pace, and was tearing through the bush before Hamilton had jumped the first fence of the plantation, and, guided by certain sounds of anguish, came up with his subordinate. Bones was standing, legs wide apart, arms akimbo, glaring down at a writhing, terror-stricken man on the ground.

He did not display any apparent wound, and Hamilton frowned questioningly at the other.

"Little toe," said Bones briefly, and yet in his very terseness conveying a hint of annoyance. "And I aimed for the *big* toe!" he added later. "I must have that naughty old rifle corrected. It isn't like me to make a perfectly ghastly error like that, old Ham − you know Bones!"

Hamilton ignored the opening. "What happened?" he asked, and at that moment Sanders came through the trees, a sporting rifle under his arm.

He listened as Bones described his exact position before the hut, his occupation, his tendency to sneeze forward, his emotions at the sight of the arrow. His first thoughts, his alacrity, his amazing presence of mind and marksmanship. When he had finished, Sanders looked at the stricken man.

"Speak: Why did you do this evil thing?"

"Lord, that is my mystery." *

Sanders jerked his head on one side and looked at the assassin through narrowed lids.

"If I hang you, what of your mystery then?" he asked, and the man made no reply.

---

* "Mystery" and "secret" are synonymous terms in the Lamongo tongue.

They put the would-be murderer in irons and confined him to the guard-room.

"I don't understand it," said the troubled Sanders. "This fellow is Akasava and, though the Akasava are by nature and inclination assassins, they have never come to headquarters to carry out their dirty work. Have steam in the *Zaire*, Hamilton, and warn your men to be ready."

"It may be some friend of his late majesty," suggested Hamilton, but Sanders shook his head.

"One king is as good as another to the Akasava," he said.

"But why Bones?" said Hamilton, and Bones smiled sadly.

"It's perhaps dawnin' on your fusty old brain, dear old Ham, that the indigenous native is slowly wakin' up to the sense of proportion, dear old sir and superior. You can't kid the jolly old native, Ham. He knows who's important an' who isn't important. He strikes at the keystone of administration, dear old bird – not that I'd disparage the importance of our blessed old excellency – "

"I'd hate to deceive you, Bones," said Sanders, with his rare smile, "but I hardly think that it is your importance that made you the object of attack – you happened to be in sight – so you got it."

For once Sanders was wrong.

Bones went to his hut that night, after inspecting the loose cordon of sentries he had posted, and getting into his pyjamas went to bed without the least suspicion that his claim was in any way justified. Bones was ordinarily a heavy sleeper and addicted to snoring – a practice which he strenuously denied.

His bed was in the centre of a large and airy hut, and there were two big windows, which were open day and night except for the frame of thin netting placed to keep out midnight insects.

It was a burning sensation on his wrist that woke him with a snort. He rubbed the sore place and diagnosed the cause as mosquitoes. The hut was full of them, and he could hear the low buzzing of insects. He was out of bed instantly, slipping his feet into his long, pliable mosquito boots.

A glance at the nearest window revealed the fact that the netting was gone, and even as he looked he saw, against the dim light, a stealthy hand creep up and then a head.

"*Twing!*"

The arrow zipped past him, and he heard the thud of it as it struck the bed.

Bones crossed the hut noiselessly and slipped his automatic from its holster.

Twice he fired, and, flinging open the door, ran out. A killing spear grazed his shoulder, and he fired again. He saw a man fall and another disappear into the darkness. Presently came a shot from the other side of the square – a sentry had seen the flying figure and had fired.

"Another Akasava," said Sanders, the first to reach the spot.

He turned over the limp figure that lay huddled against a verandah post. The second man sprawled on the square with a pistol bullet through his thigh, and he also was of the same people – the third man had escaped.

At dawn the *Zaire* pushed out into the river. Day and night she steamed, stopping only to gather wood to feed her boilers. In the darkness, the villagers on the river saw her pass, a banner of sparks floating from her two funnels, and the *lokalis* sent word through the night that there was war – for the *Zaire* never steamed at night between the treacherous shoals unless the spears were out.

The wooden drum carried news to others more interested, and ten miles short of the Akasava city, where the river narrows to pass through a sheer gorge, a cloud of arrows fell upon the deck, wounding a soldier and missing the steersman by a miracle.

The *Zaire* panted forward, for here the river runs at seven knots, and whilst the marksmen peppered the edge of the bluff, Sanders examined the arrow heads.

"Tetanus,[*] I think," he said, and knew just how serious was the situation, for the Akasava did not usually poison their arrows.

The Akasava city was deserted, except for women and old men.

[*] There are patches of land on the river, in which the germs of lockjaw abound.

"Lord," said a trembling ancient, "Kofaba has gone to the Ochori to get his beautiful bed that Tibbetti has given to Bosambo."

"You are the father of ten fools," snarled Sanders, "for the bed of the Akasava is in my great Ghost House."

"Master, a man saw the Ghost House and it was empty, and a spy of Kofaba has seen the bed, very shining and beautiful, before the hut of Bosambo."

The *Zaire* took on a new stock of wood and went northward. Near to the edge of the Ochori country, Sanders saw a canoe paddling downstream, and pulled the steamer across the river.

In the canoe was a dead man.

"This Kofaba, the king," said the headman of the paddlers, "he was killed this morning in a great fight, for Bosambo has the help of many devils. We go to bury Kofaba in the middle island, according to our custom."

Later Sanders met the main body of the routed army and stopped their canoes, only to collect their spears and arrest the petty chiefs who were in charge.

And each told him the story of Bosambo and his bed of brass.

"I cannot understand it," he said puzzled, "the Akasava would not make war on a rumour which Bosambo set in circulation that he had their infernal bed."

The shadows were lengthening when he came at last to the Ochori city, and so unexpected was the arrival, that Bosambo was unaware of his coming until Sanders strode up the main street.

He came within sight of the king's hut and stopped dead.

Before the hut, and surrounded by his admiring people, Bosambo sat in state. His throne was a brass bedstead, over the slats of which skins had been spread.

It was a bedstead of great beauty, having four glittering knobs, one at each corner, and on the headrail were shining medallions that caught the light of the setting sun and sent it back in a thousand gleaming rays.

"Oh, Bosambo, I see you," said Sanders, and the big man scrambled to his feet.

"Lord," he said hastily, "these Akasava men are thieves, for they came into my land with their spears to steal my beautiful bed."

"So I observe," said Sanders grimly, "but now you will tell your strong men to carry the bed to my ship, for did you not tell the Akasava that by magic you had taken this beautiful bedstead from the House of Ghosts?"

The agitation of Bosambo was pitiful to see. "Lord, I told them this in jest. But this bed I bought from Halli, and, lord, I spent a great fortune, paying with real silver dollars that I had saved."

"You may have the money back again," said Sanders, and Bosambo's eyes lit up, "for if you take a bedstead by magic, you may take money."

Bosambo spread out his hands in resignation. "It is written," he said.

He was a good Mohammedan, and most of the silver dollars he had paid were of a dubious quality. Mr Halley discovered this later.

A LOVER OF DOGS

The mail-boat had come into sight, had dropped its letter-bag, and was a smudge on the horizon. Sanders sorted the personal mail, putting the letters beside each plate at the breakfast-table, and Captain Hamilton of the Houssas had read three letters, a balance-sheet, and the circular of a misguided racing tipster (this was sent on from Hamilton's club), and was re-reading one of the letters for the second time when Sanders asked: "Where on earth is Bones?"

"Bones, sir?"

Hamilton looked round resentfully at the vacant chair.

"Curious," he said. "He's usually waiting on the mat for the post. Just now he is learning accountancy through a correspondence course, and that makes him keener."

Lieutenant Tibbetts, known by all and sundry, from His Excellency the Administrator to the least clerk of the district, as "Bones," took correspondence courses as a hypochondriac takes physic. They were mostly of American origin, and they emanated from colleges which, although they occupied only one small room on the nineteenth floor of important buildings, did not hesitate to print pictures of the whole of those important buildings on their notepaper. They also awarded diplomas and degrees that were imposing and grand. Bones, after three years of frenzied study, was a Doctor of Law (University of Tuxedo), a Graduate of Science (Ippikosh University), a Fellow of the Incorporated Society of Architects (of Elma, III.), and Master of Dramatic and Cinematographic Art (Spicy's College of Dramaturgy, Sacramento, Cal.).

"Maybe," said Hamilton thoughtfully, "this course will teach him to add. The last returns we rendered to HQ have been returned twice because Bones mixed the hundreds with the thousands."

"Ham! Ham! Dear old officer!"

It was the voice of Lieutenant Tibbetts, alternately shrill with excitement and hoarse with pride, and it came from outside. Hamilton got up and walked to the door, Sanders following.

Bones was standing before the broad steps, an angular figure in white, his big topee pushed back from his streaming forehead, one skinny arm extended stiffly.

"Jumping Moses!" gasped Hamilton. "Where did you get that?"

Straining at a lead wound round and round the extended hand of Bones, was the largest and ugliest bulldog he had ever seen. It was white save for a smear of black that ran across its face. Its teeth were bare, its bow legs planted determinedly, and its stub of tail quivered ecstatically.

"Bought it, old boy! Had it sent out by a jolly old pal of mine. Ah, naughty, naughty Hector!"

Hector had suddenly leapt about and was confronting Bones, his lips curled back, a strange green light in his eyes.

"Hector, Hector!" reproved Bones. "Naughty, naughty old bow-wow. Yes, you is! You'se a naughty old bow-wow!"

The naughty old bow-wow made a menacing noise.

"Now, now!" said Bones soothingly, and stooped to pat the bullet head. Hector watched the approach of the hand with suspicion and doubt, but apparently was prepared to submit to the caress.

Then: "Snap!"

Bones leapt back with a yell. "Naughty, naughty!" he squeaked. "You bad, savage, naughty boy. Ugh! I'm ashamed of you!"

Hector bared his teeth and seemed crouching for a leap.

"You'd never think, dear old Ham," beamed the proud owner, standing at a respectful distance, "that a ferocious old johnny like Hector was as gentle as a jolly young baby?"

"I shouldn't: what the dickens are you going to do with him?" asked Hamilton.

"Train him, dear old thing. In three months Hector will be carrying my stick and standing to attention. Up, Hector! Watch him, Ham! Most wonderful intelligence, dear old sir. Watch him stand on his hind legs – taught him in five minutes! Up, Hector!"

Bones snapped frantic fingers above the bull pup's head, but Hector did no more than leer at him and make a mental calculation. Could he get those fingers if he jumped? Reluctantly he decided he couldn't, and closed his eyes wearily.

Hamilton was looking at the dog. "I don't think I should call her Hector, Bones," he said drily. "Helen of Troy would be more respectful," and Bones gaped.

"Is he a she, dear old thing? Bless my dear old life! So he is. Hi, Helen! Up, Helen!"

But not even her changed status affected the dozing Helen, and in the end Bones tied her to the verandah rail and went in to breakfast.

"I got him as a surprise for you, dear old Ham," he said. "Your birthday coming along – how the dear old years spin round!"

"If you think you're going to pass that savage beast on to me – think again!" said Hamilton firmly. "My birthday was celebrated two months ago, as you know."

"Christmas coming along," said Bones pleadingly. "You're not going to turn down dear old Santa Claus, Ham?"

Sanders, a silent and an amused observer, intervened.

"It is something of a coincidence that your lady friend should have arrived today, Bones – by the way, I should keep Helen locked up whilst Fobolo is here…"

★ ★ ★

Running from the great river is a stream, so small and so covered by weed and elephant grass that only a few men knew the secret of its course. Therefore is it called "No river-One River," or, more intimately, N'ba, which is an abbreviation of ten words signifying "The-River-that-the-N'gombi-found-and-the-Isisi-lost." Which is a name of reproach, for the Isisi are riverain folk, and the N'gombi are forest people who are so unwise in the ways of water that, when they fall into the river, they make a noise that sounds like "glub glub!" and drown.

Cala cala in those days when Lieutenant Tibbetts was a comparative newcomer to the river, there lived at the end of this river of no appearance, and at the place where it drains the big lake, a man whose name was Fobolo. He was a rich man with many huts and many wives, and two and twenty young children. Of all men of the N'gombi people he was most respected and feared, for his father, Kulaba, had been a very wise man and was skilled in the way of poisons, and many inconvenient people lay in shallow holes on the islands, troublesome no more, because of the bitter foods they had taken from their wives' hands. These they had eaten, and had died, and their wives had girded their flanks with green leaves, and had stamped and strutted ceremoniously through the village in the Death Dance.

Kulaba grew rich and taught his son Fobolo his mysteries, such as how a certain blue flower may be boiled and the drippings of its steam collected; and how the bulb of an ugly weed might be mashed and its juice disposed of. And such things.

Fobolo listened attentively, and one night he went out into the forest and found a little flowering weed that has a strong and unpleasant perfume. The flowers of these he collected, and stewed them until the water was all boiled away, and then he took the mess and made a small ball of it. That night his father had pains in the stomach and died, and Fobolo took all his wealth and his younger women, and went to the edge of the lake to enjoy the reward of his experiment, praising all the time the wisdom of his father, who had said "this weed that grows flowers is death *mongo*."

So he became more powerful in the land than chiefs and headmen, and even the little kings came to him secretly and took away with them the messes he brewed. For kings have enemies.

About Fobolo's huts grew the huts of his kinsmen, and of stray fishermen who, having no village of their own, were drawn into communion by the magnet of Fobolo's greatness.

Fobolo was gaunt and tall and greedy. Wealth bred in him a desire for wealth. Though his deeply dug stores were filled with ivory teeth and rubber, and under the floor of his hut were many thousands of brass rods, and salt and other treasures were stacked tight in his huts, he sought new means of profit.

On a cold, clear morning, when only the stars were hot in the sky, a woman in the house of the Akasava king went shivering into the open with a blanket about her shoulders. She knelt before the dead fire and blew at the ashes until the air was filled with snowy specks, and when she had coaxed the fire to a proper redness and had set a pot upon it and filled that pot with water and corn, she went to carry food to the king's dogs. They did not greet her with thin yelps, nor tear frantically at their grass-walled compound at the sound of her feet.

There was a silence that was strange and alarming. As she stood peering into the void, the stars went out in the sky and the sun shot up and she saw in the light the dogs were gone, and went, coughing and sobbing in terror, to the king's hut.

"O shameful and ugly woman," said the king, naked and blinking in the light to which he had been called, "did I not give to your care my fine dogs, and now they are gone?"

"Lord," she whimpered, "last night I gave them water and dried fish, and they were happy, one putting out his tongue at me, and all moving their tails from side to side, which is the way dogs speak."

Ten minutes later a well-beaten woman howled her misery, and the *lokalis* of the city were drumming the news of the great steal.

It would seem that N'Kema the king was not the only loser. For the chief of the Isisi village, which lay on the other bank of the river, came paddling furiously to the Akasava beach and stalked into the presence of the king.

"Lord king, there is sorrow in my stomach that I should tell you this: last night came your young men to my village and took from me two beautiful fat dogs that were ready for the marriage feast of my own son. And these dogs were each worth five and five bags of salt."

Forcibly and with violence did the king deny the charge.

"It seems, little chief that, having stolen my dogs, you come to me with a lie that your dogs are taken. If I had lived in the days of my fathers before Sandi came, I would cut out your tongue and give your body to the ghosts. But now I will go to Sandi and tell him, and he shall put iron rings and chains on your legs according to his law."

Sanders at that time was on the *Zaire*, making a tour of inspection, and to him they went and with them four smaller chiefs of the neighbourhood who had suffered loss. And small comfort they received.

A few months later, the youngest wife of N'Kema was seen by his favourite daughter, Militi, who was the apple of the king's eye, speaking with a lover in the forest. And Militi carried word to her father, hating the woman who had replaced her mother in favouritism.

"This woman of yours has a quiet man," she said, and told him things that a woman of fourteen would not have understood had she been white.

N'Kema took his youngest wife by the nape of her neck and flogged her with a strip of hippohide – which hurts.

In his absence on a hunting trip, the wife found her way through the hidden river and came to Fobolo's village.

"I see you, wife of N'Kema, the king," greeted Fobolo, standing on the beach as she landed.

"I see you, Fobolo: I have a riddle for you."

"No man understands riddles better than I," said Fobolo. "Tell me this, and I will give you an answer."

"When the young she-leopard claws," said the woman, giving him her mystery, "must you wait for the scratches to heal and then go forth and be clawed again?"

"My answer to your riddle is this," said Fobolo, who had solved such enigmas before, "that it is better that the leopard should die that he will claw no more."

This clawing leopard was a popular illustration in a land where the favour of men is shown by a ring of brass, and their displeasure is scored deeply on the shoulders of their women.

Whilst Fobolo went into his house, the woman wandered along the beach. And she came at last to a compound on the wooded promontory where there were many dogs. And two at least she recognised.

She went back to the beach before Fobolo's hut, and after a while he came to her empty-handed.

"Woman," he said, "this is in my mind. That little leopards may die and nobody shall speak. But if the leopard be great, then shall everybody speak and say, 'Last night this leopard was alive: today he is dead,' and then Sandi will come and there will be a palaver and perhaps a woman who talks, and Fobolo's hut will be fire and he will be a ghost in the trees. Therefore, go back to your leopard and let him scratch."

Shamelessly he retained the present she had brought him.

The wife of the king went home sick with fright, and that night when her husband returned she told him a lie.

"Lord, this day I went fishing through the River-that-the-N'gombi-found, and there I saw Fobolo with many dogs. And of these there were two which were like the fat man dog Cheepi that you loved."

It was the very worst luck for all concerned that Bosambo, paramount chief of the Ochori, should have taken into his head the idea of paying a state visit to the Isisi king at that particular moment. N'Kema, with two war canoes, had put out from his beach *en route* to recover his stolen dogs, when Bosambo's flotilla swept into sight round the bend of the river. With Bosambo were fifty excellent spearsmen, for the chief of the Ochori was by no means certain that the invitation which the Isisi had extended to him was purely disinterested.

At the sight of Bosambo's painted canoes, N'Kema and his fellows stopped paddling, for Bosambo was notoriously a creature of Sandi, and it was essential for N'Kema's peace of mind that his affair with the dog-stealer should be settled without publicity.

He had hoped that the canoes would pass, but Bosambo was a man with very keen eyesight.

"I see you, N'Kema," he boomed as his canoe drew alongside the others. "Is there war or peace in this land, that you go out with your young spearsmen?"

"Bosambo, I came out to meet you, for, as you know, the people of the Akasava love you. And besides, I am going to the Great Lake to fish."

"It seems to me," said Bosambo, "that I see many shields at the bottom of your canoes. Now, tell me this, N'Kema: do men fish with shields?"

Whereupon Mr N'Kema, who lacked the natural gift of lying, spoke frankly of the outrage which had been committed, and of his desire to execute summary justice upon the robber.

"I will see this Fobolo," said Bosambo instantly. "And be sure, N'Kema, that justice will be done. For, as you know, we men of the Ochori do not eat dogs; therefore it is certain that we shall return all we find."

N'Kema knew this to be true. For some extraordinary reason, to the Southern Ochori people dog meat was taboo.

"But, Bosambo," he protested, "how may you know which are my beautiful dogs if I am not there to call them by loving words, and tell you that this is mine and this is not mine?"

"And if you say that all are yours," said Bosambo, "how do I know that you speak the truth? N'Kema, I will go alone and hold a palaver, and in the end word of this matter will be sent to Sandi, who judges all, like God."

Bosambo, who had an amazing knowledge of the country, found the Little River without difficulty, and at the noon hour, when Fobolo was asleep in the shadow of his hut, Bosambo came to him and there was a long palaver, which could end only in one way.

A carrier pigeon had taken to Sanders a sketchy account of Bosambo's rough-and-ready justice. Later came Fobolo himself full of trouble and plaints. Squatting in the hot sunlight before the residency, Fobolo told his story.

"Lord, this Bosambo came and made a long palaver, saying many evil things against me."

"Tell me what evil things, Fobolo," said Sanders.

"Lord, he called me a stealer of dogs and an eater of dogs; and that was foolish, as your lordship knows, for all true men eat dogs. And then, lord, when the palaver was finished, Bosambo went to a certain place near the water, where I keep all my dogs, and he took them all away with him; and, lord, they sat in Bosambo's canoe and made sad noises."

Sanders thought a moment, his chin in his palm, and then: "Fobolo, I speak! As to these dogs, I will send a book to Bosambo, and he shall tell me where they have gone. Afterwards you shall tell me from whence they came."

"Lord," protested the other, "they are my very own dogs. I have had them all since they were little babies – "

"That is as may be," said Sanders. "Now listen, Fobolo. Strange stories come to me from the Upper River of men who die quickly, and for no reason. And my spies tell me of women who go secretly to you by night, and come away with little gourds which hold death. Some day I will come to your village and hold a palaver. Tell me, Fobolo, how high do the trees grow on the edge of the Great Lake?"

Fobolo shuddered. "Lord, they are too high for me," he said huskily.

"But not so high that one of my soldiers cannot climb," replied Sanders significantly. "And on one branch to fasten a rope where a man can hang. I think, Fobolo, your days are very few."

That night Fobolo sat with his followers in that place on the edge of the residency wood which is set apart for the entertainment of such visitors as he; and in the morning he was gone.

The disappearance of Helen was not discovered till daylight. Bones had made for her a kennel of a peculiarly ingenious type. It was an exact replica of his own hut, with verandah poles and thatched roof complete. He had made it with the assistance of half the garrison, and had covered the floor of the interior with a thick layer of native grass. And Helen seemed to be satisfied, and to have no other desire than to sleep.

She had been attached to a thick leather thong, which in turn was fastened to one of the verandah poles, and there, with a large bone and a dish of water, Bones had left her, apparently reconciled to her fate, and even looking forward to the coming day. And in the morning she was gone.

"Nobody but an imbecile would fasten a bulldog to a leather lead," said Hamilton. "Of course she gnawed it through."

"But, my dear old thing," said Bones dismally, "she was so perfectly satisfied when I said 'night-night' to her. And she looked up into my eyes with a kind of resigned, happy look, and toddled off without a word."

"You're bringing tears to my eyes," said Hamilton. "And now she has toddled off without a word again. You'll probably find her in the woods."

A search, conducted by the entire population, produced no sign of the fugitive. Bones, looking for clues, found nothing more tangible than one of his slippers in the darkest corner of the kennel. It was half-eaten.

Curiously enough, nobody associated the disappearance of Helen of Troy with Fobolo, and no word of Helen came from the spies of Sanders.

Three months later, Fobolo called together his kinsmen and spoke to them.

"You know that I am rich and that all men envy me, even Sandi, who sent Bosambo here to take my dogs, which he has sold to the chiefs of the Isisi. And now I have word that Sandi is coming with his soldiers because of the death of a certain man who was poisoned by his wife. I must go quickly, or I shall hang, for the woman was put to the fire by the king of the Akasava, and she said that she bought the poison from me, giving me a thousand brass *matakos*. And this is true, that she told me it was for a leopard who broke into her garden and scratched her. But because N'Kema hates me, he has sent word to Sandi — and it will not be good to stay. Tonight we will go away into the forest, taking our women and our treasures, and the dog with the beautiful face that I found in Sandi's garden. Also will we take Militi, who is the favourite daughter of the king, and is the most beautiful woman in the land. And she shall dance for us, and the king will be sorry."

That night, when the *Zaire* was threshing her way up between the shoals, and was within ten miles of the Akasava city, Fobolo and his kinsmen landed noiselessly on the beach, and, slaying the sentry before the hut of the king's daughter, carried her away, and within two hours came to the village by the lake.

"Now, woman," said Fobolo, "you may cry, but none will hear you."

The girl, an object of dispassionate interest on the part of Fobolo's wives, lay moaning on the ground, more dead than alive, for Fobolo had choked her into silence when he carried her off. His kinsmen and his people were ready, their cooking-pots upon their shoulders, their young goats and dogs tethered, and each carried something of his treasures. Fobolo went to the little compound on the headland and opened the grass door.

"Come, my pretty one," he said.

Helen of Troy opened her eyes and blinked at the sunlight. Then she stretched both her hind legs and her forelegs and yawned. For three months she had lain in that roomy pen, waddling out at intervals to inspect the village, and never once in all that time had she shown the slightest indication of her true character.

To Fobolo, Helen of Troy was a normal dog, something which in time would make an excellent *pièce de résistance* for a feast. And Helen had fostered this illusion, for she had been content to eat and sleep, and since, after the native way, none interfered with her, she had interfered with none. Obediently and meekly she trotted at Fobolo's heels back to the village street, where the carriers were waiting. The girl still sat huddled, clasping her knees, her face hidden.

"Come, woman," said Fobolo, "for you will walk far before you sleep."

So far he got, when his trained ears heard the rumble of a distant *lokali*. *Lokalis* belong to the night and to the early morning, when the air is still and sound travels fastest. He bent his head and listened, then suddenly heaved a long, sobbing sigh.

"Sandi is coming," he said. "I think we had better go."

In his hand was a long and pliant thong. He dropped it sharply across the girl's shoulders and jerked her to her feet.

"Walk, woman," he said.

And at that moment Helen of Troy began to take a serious interest in the proceedings.

At the shriek of the girl she growled softly; and as though encouraged by the ferocity of her own language, the growl became a bark the like of which had never been heard by Fobolo. The fat food dogs looked round at Helen in terror. That bark stirred something within them, and they whimpered fiercely in response.

"Dog," said Fobolo, "be silent."

He brought up the thong and it fell once. He only knew one kind of dog – a dog that whimpered and fled. But Helen did neither. She stood square, motionless, glaring, her black lips curled in a silent snarl.

"Let us go," said Fobolo.

And then something weighing about 20 lbs leapt at him. He struck it down with the bunch of spears he carried on his shield arm, but the respite was temporary.

As the *Zaire* pushed her nose through the last barrier of weeds and gained the open water of the Lake, Sanders saw a figure running along the sandy edge of the lake. He was running at a speed which at once interested and startled the Commissioner. Behind him bounded a small white speck.

"What is that, Bones?"

Bones focussed his glasses. "Looks like a man running to me, sir," he said.

At that moment the flying native saw the *Zaire*, and, turning, plunged into the water and swam frantically toward the boat. Behind him came a blunt head, and, at a short interval, the white stump of a tail.

They hauled the two on board together, which was necessary, since Helen of Troy had gripped his loincloth and was not to be shaken off.

"Dogs I know," gasped Fobolo. "Men eat them. But it is not right that dogs should eat men. I think this is a devil. Devils also I have seen, being a wise man, but none like this."

"My man," said Sanders, "there are other devils to be seen. And if in your village I find Militi, the daughter of N'Kemo, this night you shall live with ghosts."

THE CAMERA MAN

For a thousand years (which may only mean a few centuries) there had been a feud between the Leopards and the Fire Ghosts. When the Leopards came under the ban of civilised administration, and soldiers of all nations penetrated the hinterlands with judges and priests and commissioners who were something of both, and by whipping and summary hanging, stamped down this most evil of all secret societies, the Fire Ghosts, being comparatively innocuous, were left supreme. For they did not hunt young maidens having gloves on their hands shaped like leopards' paws, with little steel knives in place of the claws, nor did they hold terrible meetings where things were done that can only be described in highly technical books. They were mild folk who believed in ghosts and devils, and they did no more than chop an occasional enemy and paint the soles of their feet with his blood.

But presently they, too, came under the ban, and dwindled until all the ancient hates and animosities, together with the secrets of their rituals, were concentrated in the villages of Labala and Busuri, and although they were within a dozen miles of one another, they kept the peace.

Then a thing happened that had no parallel in history. A woman of Busuri married Obaga, the hunter of Labala. As to the reason for this monstrous union, some say one thing and some say another. They first met in the forest, and each made the contemptuous gesture – by European standards vulgar – with which Labala and Busuri greet one another. Then they met again and refrained. Afterwards they smiled, and then came Obaga to the Chief of the Busuri and the father of the

95

girl, and a bargain was struck. So M'Libi of Busuri went into the hut of Obaga and lived with him for two years, but bore him no children.

Whereupon all the old women of the village put their shaven heads together and cackled joy that their prophecies had been fulfilled, for they had said that no children could come of such an unnatural marriage. So also the old women of Labala spoke over their menial tasks and cursed the day that such a likeable girl had gone to the Fire Ghosts. So affairs went on, Obaga patient, uncomplaining, kindly. He brought her the finest of his pelts; the noblest of monkey tails, the prerogative of chiefs, were split to make her a bed robe. A few gibed him secretly because he was loved; none openly because he was feared, for he threw spears unerringly and had no regard for human life.

Then on a day, Obaga returned from a hunting trip seven days earlier than he had expected. More important, he was not expected by his handsome young wife. Obaga found his hut empty, and when he came out with knit brows, N'kema, the fisherman, shouted a jest that had to do with the short memories of women.

Without a word Obaga went back into his hut and gathered the short killing spears he had put aside, polished them with dust gathered from before his hut, and, sitting on his bed, whetted one of them for two hours until the edge of it was razor-sharp. Then he went forth, twirling the spear between his fingers. He was making for the banks of a little river which runs through a wood, for this was a notorious meeting-place for lovers of a kind. Therefore, it was called The Wood of Changed Hearts – or so we may translate it, though the stomach is more readily recognised as the seat of all emotion.

Somebody had gone to warn M'Libi, and halfway to the wood, very near to a patch of shallow graves (these Northern Ochori considering it unlucky to carry their dead across water to the middle islands) he found her sitting on a fungus-grown trunk of dead wood, her hands crossed on her breast. The scowl on her face denied her humility.

"O M'Libi, I see you," said Obaga the hunter softly, and she set her white teeth for all that was to come, her eyes fixed on the bright spear blade which glittered and flashed in the afternoon sun.

"Obaga, I have been to the woods to gather leaves for mourning, for my brother has died this day in the Ochori city, and Bosambo sent word to me."

"Many things have died this day," said Obaga. He held his spear at full arm's length by his thigh, and he so spun it with finger and thumb, that the blade was a blur of light. This was a trick of his when he was not sure in his mind, and she knew it well and took courage.

"When I was born," she said slowly, her eyes never leaving the spear, "it was said that I should have two lives; one of greatness and one of evilness. Out of the mud grows the wonderful flower. Obaga, who knows what will come from this mud?"

The hunter wetted his lips with the tip of his tongue.

"Who is this lover of yours?" he asked her, and for the first time her eyes left the spear.

"If there is to be killing, begin!" she said, and dropped her hands to the tree trunk.

"There will be no killing," said Obaga. "Come."

She followed him back to the village, and, to the disappointment of all, there was neither killing nor beating. At dawn next day, Obaga gathered his spears, his bows and loose-headed monkey arrows, girded a broad-bladed elephant sword about his waist, and went back to his hunting. His wife stood and watched him until he was out of sight. One other watched from the fringe of the forest, Tebeli, the boaster, and when he had made sure that the husband was gone, he hurried to M'Libi.

★ ★ ★

There can be no question that Bones had an inquiring mind. And there was a special reason why he should be interested in photography and all that pertained to the art, at that moment.

"You stick your infernal nose into every darned thing that doesn't concern you," said the wrathful Hamilton, the owner of a new camera, an important plate of which Bones had irretrievably ruined. "I've been waiting for weeks to get that cloud effect over the sea, and you, like the howling jackass…"

"Not howlin', dear old Ham," murmured the patient Bones, his eyes tightly shut, "quiet, dignified, sufferin', dear old savage, in silence…not howlin'."

"I told you…" spluttered Hamilton.

"You told me nothin'," said Bones gently, "and a boy should be told. I read it somewhere in a jolly old book the other day, a boy should be told how to work the shutter and everything. A loaded camera, dear old tyro – which means a cove that doesn't know an awful lot – a loaded camera is worse than a loaded gun. Listen to the voice of reason, dear old Ham, the *vox reasoni*. I picked up the silly old thing and clicked the shutter –"

"Never leave things within reach of children," said Hamilton bitterly.

Bones shrugged his lean shoulders. "Dear, but explosive old officer," he said quietly, "there may be method in my jolly old naughtiness. There may be money, dear old improvident one. Old Bones may be working out a great old scheme in his nippy old nut, to make us all rich."

"Orange growing?" asked Hamilton pointedly, and Bones writhed. Once he had conceived a get-rich-quick scheme, and Hamilton had put his money into an orange syndicate which Bones had conceived. They had imported trees and they had grown trees that bore everything except oranges. Some had borne apples, a few might, had they lived, have borne chestnuts. Bones bought the young trees by post, from the Zeizermann Mail Order Corporation – the proprietors of which are still in Sing Sing.

"Being my superior officer, sir and captain, you may taunt me," he said stiffly and shrugging his shoulders again, saluted and went back to his quarters. He could, of course, have offered a very complete and satisfactory explanation, but had he done so, he would have spoilt the surprise he had in store for everybody.

And to Bones, surprise (other people's pleasant surprise) was the joy of life.

Most of his daydreams were about surprises that he sprung on other people. Bones had on many occasions owned a potential Derby winner, and on the morning of the race, the jockey having proved false, Bones had donned the colours and to the amazement of his friends and the confusion of his sinister enemies, he had ridden the horse home a winner in a desperate finish.

"Never in the history of this great classic (so his dream *Sporting Life* read) has there been a more wonderful exhibition of masterly jockeyship than that given by the famous amateur rider, Captain (or Major) Tibbetts. He is a noble-looking fellow, with grave blue eyes and a mask-like yet mobile face…"

At this point Bones would sigh happily and introduce The Girl. There was always a girl. He saw her on the stand, white-faced and tearing at her handkerchief (not an expensive handkerchief) or clutching at her throat, and she always fell into his arms when he dismounted, and, presumably, was weighed in with him.

He had surprised the War Office by inventing a new gun and the Admiralty by compounding a new strategy, but mostly, as has been remarked before, he surprised girls by his strength, genius, workmanship, knowledge of women, kindness of disposition, tenderness of heart, wit, nobility of character, and general all-round excellence. And the motif of Bones' plan of surprisement at the moment was an amazing cinema camera which he had seen advertised in an American magazine, and which at that moment was speeding on its way – it would in fact arrive by the same steamer that carried home Father Carrelli.

Bones had an immense faith in the probity of magazine advertisements, and when he read of Keissler's King Kamera which was offered at $150.00, and after he had discovered that $150.00 was not fifteen thousand, but a hundred and fifty and no cents, he wrote for the prospectus and received in reply an avalanche of literature which was alone worth the money.

Therefore, anything of a photographic nature meant much to Bones. He could have explained his fault in a word. Instead he maintained silence. There was time enough later – and the story had to be written, for in those days the picture play was coming to its own, and Bones was an enthusiastic subscriber to all movie periodicals that were published. He had many stories in his mind.

Nobody paid any particular attention to the arrival of a large case or of sundry other bulky packages, because both Sanders and Hamilton had long since ceased to wonder at the amazing character of Bones' mail. He had, on an average, one new hobby a month, and the inauguration of each was signalised by mails of terrific or mysterious proportions.

The first hint Hamilton had that something unusual was afoot, came to him in the nature of a shock. One afternoon he strolled over to the hut in which Bones had his headquarters, and, as was usual, he made straight for the big window which gave access to the young man's sitting-room; and, looking in, he gasped.

Sitting at the table was a young man who was not Bones. His face was a bright and vivid yellow; his hands and bare arms were similarly tinted; about his eyes were two rings of blue. Hamilton stared open-mouthed, and then dashed into the hut through the door.

"For heaven's sake, what's the matter with you, Bones – fever?"

Bones looked up with a horrible smile, for his lips were painted a blue that was nearly purple.

"Get into bed at once," ordered Hamilton. "I'll wire through to Administration to get a doctor down – you poor young devil!"

Bones looked at him haughtily as he fixed a slight, dark moustache to his upper lip. And then it was that Hamilton saw the make-up box and the mirror.

"What are you doing, you great jackass?" he asked, offensive in his relief.

"Just a bit of make-up, dear old audience."

"Make-up? Yellow? What are you supposed to be? The King of the Gold Coast?"

"That's who I'm supposed to be," said Bones carelessly, and handed a slip of paper to his visitor.

"Reginald de Coursy, a man of synister appearance, yet of plesing apearance. His eyes show sings of diserpation dissipation disapation his nose is aquerline his mouth creul. He looks like a man who has lived."

"Is that you?" asked Hamilton.

Bones nodded.

"You look more like a man who has died," snarled his superior. "What's the meaning of this dashed nonsense?"

He did not say "dashed." Bones screwed up his face in an expression of pain, and the grimace made his face even more startling.

"Language, dear old thing! That's one of the things I'm not going to have. I hate to hurt your jolly old feelings, Ham, but the studio *must* be kept clean."

"Studio?"

"Well, I haven't got a studio yet," admitted Bones, "but that's coming, dear old Felix – you're Felix."

"I'm what?" asked the dazed Hamilton.

Bones searched the litter of papers by the side of his make-up box and found another slip, which he handed without a word to his chief.

"Fellix Harington a young and hansom fellow of 26. His countenance is open and Frank and a genal smile is in his eyes, but very deceptful."

Hamilton could only look helplessly from the paper to Bones. That gentleman was perfectly composed.

"There's a fortune in it, my dear old officer," he said calmly. "In fact, there's two fortunes in it. Now, my idea is a play where a seemingly villainous person turns out a jolly old hero in the end.

101

And the seemingly heroic old person turns out a jolly old rotter – robs his old father, and is going to murder him, when up comes Reggie the Knut – that's me."

"Wait a minute," said the dazed Hamilton. "Do I understand that you have cast me for this part – and may I ask who is the father?"

"The jolly old Commissioner," said Bones complacently, and Hamilton's jaw dropped.

When he recovered command of his voice: "Do you imagine that Sanders is going to jigger about, wearing false whiskers, just to amuse an infernal – "

"I'm not sure about the whiskers," said Bones thoughtfully, "I've been turning it over in my mind, dear old Ham, and I'm not so sure that the whiskers would come out. A little beard perhaps, or maybe a couple of mutton chops."

Then Bones' scheme came out. He had written a great play; it was entirely without women characters. He, Sanders and Hamilton were to act the story in their spare time, work in, to use his own expression, "a dinky little battle between savages, where I come along, dear old thing, and foil them single-handed – and it will be a sensation, Ham. There's never been anything done like it and there never will be again perhaps, unless I do it. Look at the life, my dear old Felix…the wonderful scenery…it will be a sensation, dear old thing. I wouldn't be surprised if we didn't make half-a-million."

Sanders heard all about this new scheme of Bones' without being either annoyed or perturbed.

"But you may tell him from me, Hamilton, that under no conditions will I act the fool in front of his wretched camera. By the way, did you see it?"

Hamilton nodded. "It's not a bad-looking camera," he admitted, "and Bones can turn the handle very well. He's been to the kitchen, practising on the knife-cleaner, and he says he's got exactly the right speed."

Baffled in his great attempt to create a picture which should startle the world, Bones, the adaptable, decided upon a great native drama.

"It's never been done, dear old Ham," he said eagerly one night at dinner, when he expounded his scheme – and it was curious how quickly he had assimilated the clichés of the studio – "that's the one thing you've got to be careful about on the cinema, old boy, do something that has never been done before. I'm working out the scenery now – "

"The word you want, I think," said Hamilton, "is 'scenario.' "

"Same thing, my dear old Ham," said Bones testily. "Good gracious heavens, why do you interrupt me on a trivial little matter like scenery? Scenery or scenario – same jolly old thing."

"Where are you laying the plot?" asked Sanders.

"Anywhere, dear old excellency," said Bones vaguely. "My idea is to make Ahmet the hero, who runs away with the beautiful Kalambala, the Sultan's favourite wife. And she's rescued by a handsome young Englishman – "

"Need you go any further?" asked Hamilton.

"A handsome young Englishman," repeated Bones, with a contemptuous glance at his superior.

"You, of course," said Hamilton.

"Anyway, she's rescued."

"And then what do you do with her?" asked Hamilton.

But Bones hadn't got as far as this. He filmed the first scene of this exciting story, and Hamilton and Sanders came down to witness the production. The attempt was a failure for many reasons. Ahmet had to stroll on to the scene, fold his arms, shake his head and smile. Then he had to shrug his shoulders and walk off. And he did it remarkably well until Bones started turning the handle.

"Roll your eyes," screamed Bones.

"Lord, I roll my eyes," said Ahmet, standing stiffly to attention and saluting.

Bones stopped turning with a groan. "O man," he said bitterly, "when I speak to you, do not stick your big feet together and salute me! Stand easy! Now try it again."

He tried it again, with no greater success; for this time, instead of saluting, Ahmet stood regimentally at ease. When the scene was made right, new trouble arose. The escaping Sultana was to be played by the wife of a Corporal Hafiz; and Corporal Hafiz refused resolutely, and with much stamping of feet and spitting on the ground, to allow his wife to be carried in Ahmet's arms.

"You're demoralising the detachment, Bones," said Hamilton sternly, and dismissed the actors to their several duties.

Bones did not speak to his company commander for two days, at the end of which time he had found a new and more alluring scheme.

"I've got it, old Ham," he said one day, dashing into the dining-room where the two men were sitting, smoking their after-luncheon cigars, in what shade they could find, for the sun was burning and there was little or no breeze from the sea.

"You'll get sunstroke if you go around without your helmet," said Hamilton lazily. "What have you got? The picture?"

"The picture!" said Bones triumphantly. "The greatest stunt ever, dear old excellency. And it all came out of jolly old Bones' nut. Lives and customs of savage old tribes, dear old officer." He stepped back to notice the effect of his words.

"Lives and customs of savage tribes?" repeated Hamilton.

"That's the idea. Wherever I go, I take the camera, and if I don't make a thousand a week lecturing on a subject, dear old killjoy, that is dear to the heart of every jolly old patriot, my name is mud."

"Your real name I've never been able to remember," said Hamilton, "but it does strike me as being much more feasible than the other."

Thereafter, Bones spent a great deal of his time filming native scenes; and for once there happened to be method in his hobby. Having trained Ahmet to turn the handle, he was able to make a personal appearance in most. Sometimes he was standing in a negligent attitude, talking to a native woman as she cooked the evening meal. In other pictures he was patting the heads of little black toddlers (after carefully fixing a handkerchief about their middles, lest the susceptibilities of Surbiton should be shocked). Sometimes he was standing with his arms folded, and a sad but determined look upon his face, on the bow of the *Zaire*. And to all he supplied titles. He showed Hamilton a list of them.

"Kindly Chief Comissioner helping Savidges to build a Hut."

Or, more flamboyantly, and in keeping with the spirit of modern subtitles:

"Far from the hum and compitetion of the bussy world, the native goes about his daily tarsks, under the watchful but bernevilent eye of the Cheif Comissioner."

"One of the advantages of the cinema," said Hamilton, "is that you needn't be able to spell. Who is this Chief Commissioner you keep talking about in your titles, Bones?" he asked, interested. "I didn't know Sanders was assisting you in your nefarious plan to pander to the debased instincts of the British public!"

Bones coughed. "Well, to be perfectly candid, dear old thing," he said, "dear old Sanders did talk about toddling down once, but he got stage-fright, old Ham. You know what these youngsters are, what, what?"

Bones could be waggish, but Bones could never be so waggish that he could lead Hamilton from his deadly trail.

"You don't mean to tell me that you're masquerading as a Commissioner? Why, even the poorest little street Arab that ever stole sixpence to go to the pictures will recognise you're fake!"

Bones could afford to smile indulgently at the other's strictures.

"What we want now, Ham," he said seriously at dinner that night, "is a jolly old war! If we could only get a real good old dust-up between the mighty N'gombi and good old Bosambo, with me in the foreground, just to show that Britain's watchful eye still keeps a watch, when naughty natives sleep – that's a good bit of poetry, by the way, dear old thing, and don't pass it off as your own."

"Bones, if you wish for war I'll kill you," said Sanders, coming in at that moment. "The territories are quiet, and if we can only get over the harvest without a real big blood-letting, I shall be a happy man."

Bones was silent, but not altogether hopeless. There was need for somebody to go to the Ochori country, for there was news of a recrudescence of Leopard trouble, and Bones gladly availed himself of the opportunity.

On the first night away from headquarters, when the *Zaire* was tied up to a wood, Private Mahmud sought out his sergeant.

"Effendi," said he in coast Arabic, "what is this small box which Tibbetti carries and which you turn with a handle? Some say that it is a new gun; others that it is a taker of pictures. Now, we know that it is not a taker of pictures, because, when Hamiltini desires that a row of Houssas shall appear upon paper – which is against the law of the Prophet – he says, 'Damnyoustandstill,' which is an English word, and makes a clicking noise. Now Tibbetti does not say 'Damnyoustandstill' for he desires that you should walk; also he turns a handle. Tell me now, Effendi, why these things happen."

Sergeant Ahmet, in all solemnity, explained as much of the mystery box as he understood.

"When Tibbetti turns the handle, pictures appear, one after another, so that when they are looked at quickly, they seem to be one and all moving."

"That is too much of a mystery for me," admitted the inquirer after knowledge, and sought no further information.

Not unconscious of his responsibility and importance, Ahmet was loth to let the discussion end there.

"Some day, when Tibbetti is away, I will gather you all together and make a special picture for you, so that your wives may see them. And for this you shall all give me one silver dollar."

Though they boggled at the dollar, his men accepted the principle of the offer.

The opportunity he sought came to them after they had left the Ochori city and were journeying up that wild bank line which the *Zaire* so seldom traversed. More definite news had reached Bones about the Leopards – not the clean and yellow thing that stalks and slays, but something vile and abominable in the shape of man. Bones became instantly soldier and representative of the law, and for the moment his heart turned from Hollywood.

★ ★ ★

Obaga came back from his hunting. He had been a month away, and he had brought with him ten bushmen carriers, each with a load of pelts, for he was a skilful and patient man. His wife met him outside the village, her hands crossed before her, token of her meekness, and he passed her without a word, though, if he had known all he was to know, he would have returned to the village alone. She made him his dinner, and served it on the palms of her two hands.

"I stay here now for three and three moons," said Obaga, "for the beasts will be breeding, and many have already gone away into their secret places."

This she expected, and by native reckoning a month would pass before he learnt the truth. That night, when her husband was sleeping the sleep of utter weariness, she crept forth from her hut, and sped secretly to the wood, where the other man was waiting, she having sent for him.

"Obaga is returned," she said. "Now, friend, what shall I do? For when he knows, he will kill me."

"Why should he know?" compromised the other, manlike. "For are you not his wife, and is he not a man? I think it is best for you to say, 'Husband, there is good news for you, and you shall have a son for your house'."

She made a sound of impatience. "He knows what he knows," she said cryptically, but to him understandably. "If I tell him this, I will take his killing spear into my hands, so that it will be sooner over. If you were to come into the hut tonight and spear him as he sleeps, or wait for him when he goes into the wood tomorrow, that would be best."

"For you, woman, but not for me," said the other. "All men in this village know that I am your lover, and Sandi will come with his guns and his soldiers, and my hut will be burnt. Also, Tibbetti is already here. He is sitting in the village of Busuri, where there is a Leopard palaver. It is said that there will be hangings. I know this, because the cunning ones have hidden their pads in the ground."

She drew a quick breath. "Bring me the pads," she whispered. "To-morrow, when it is dark, bring me the leopard pads."

He was horrified at the suggestion, but she insisted; and in trepidation and fear he left her. She went back and lay down by her man.

When the next night came, she found Tebeli, for whom she had dared so much, and he was shaking like a leaf, and in his hands were two ugly skin-shapes, with little knives in place of claws, and the hair had earth upon it, as though they had recently been dug from the ground. He dropped them into the hands she held out as though they were red hot, and, turning without a word, would have fled back towards his village, but she stopped him.

"Now, my own man, go towards Busuri, where Tibbetti is, and tell him that a Leopard walks toward the village, and that, if they wait by the path, they may take him."

He was in no mood for such an adventure, but she was stronger than he, and he went. And M'Libi returned to her hut, the pads, glove-like, on her hands. Obaga was too busy with his spears to notice, but when his eyes turned, he saw in the flickering light of the fire the hideous things she wore, and dropped his spear and leapt up with a roar.

"Woman who art shameless, what have you there?"

"These I found in my little box of wood, Obaga," she said innocently.

She held her hands up to be admired, and the rusted steel claws glittered evilly.

"Oh ko!" said Obaga, agitated, "whose things are these?"

"They belong to a man in the village of Busuri," she said. "Lobala, the fisher. These he gave to me when I was a little girl."

"Give them," said her husband, snatching them from her hand.

A second later, he was striding through the village to the forest path that led to Busuri. But the lover of his wife was quicker than he, and on the edge of the village three soldiers seized Obaga and brought him into the presence of Bones.

Now, of all things certain, this is most sure; any man who carries on his person, or hides in his hut, the insignia of the Leopard, is already dead. From one end of Africa to the other there is no mercy for the sons of the Leopard. Obaga knew that his fate was sealed.

"Man," said Bones quietly, as he surveyed the damning evidence, "what horrible things are these?"

"Lord, they were given to me to bring to the village," said Obaga.

"Who gave?" asked Bones, but the man was silent, because it was his wife who had given them.

"Lord, if I hang, I must hang," said Obaga. "But I tell you this, that the Leopards are my enemies, for my father was a Fire Ghost, and we of the village of Labala have fought Leopards for a thousand years."

Bones knew this was true, and was puzzled how a man from Labala came to be in possession of these things; and the order that should have been given for instant execution was delayed. In the morning the spies brought news from Busuri and the truth was out. Obaga, returning home, found his wife had fled.

That was the story of Obaga. There it would have ended, but for the village gossip. This matter of the Leopards cleared up to the satisfaction of everybody, save a still form that hung on a tree three miles from the village, Bones turned his thoughts to the customs and habits of native people. The artist in him had prayed that there would be a fight; the administrator in him was heartily glad that the trouble had ended without disturbance. Bones had a brilliant idea. He sent for the chief of the Busuri village and exhibited to him the camera.

"O chief," said Bones, "this is a little eye that sees and remembers, and it desires to look upon the brave Ochori in battle. Now, let your young men play for me, pretending that they are warriors of two camps, attacking one another. But this you shall tell them, that if one man hurts the other, he shall be whipped," he added hastily, knowing with what enthusiasm these spear players entered into the spirit of their exercise.

On the lower deck of the *Zaire* a troubled Sergeant Ahmet took counsel with a number of his comrades.

"Let no man speak to Tibbetti and tell him that I have turned the handle, that your faces should be in this wonderful box," he said. For, in Bones' absence, he had that day photographed his self-conscious soldiery. "Tomorrow morning, when it is light, I myself will get the pictures out of the box, for Tibbetti has told me, that all that is within there he will see. And I am a full sergeant, and he may take my stripes away."

In the light of the early morning sun, under the curious and interested eyes of his friends, he opened the camera and looked carefully, unrolling the film foot by foot.

"Now, God be thanked!" said Ahmet in his relief. "For it seems that I did not take your picture at all. There is nothing there but yellow ribbon. Let us roll it up again, so that Tibbetti shall not know."

The preparations for the great battle picture were made on an unprecedented scale. Bones rehearsed and rehearsed until his shirt stuck to his body, and then rehearsed again. And all the women and children of the village stood round, their fingers to their teeth, and watched the producer at work.

"Not there, you silly old ass!" screamed Bones in strident English. "Get over there, you silly old josser! Not there, go there! No, not there! Oh, you ditherer!"

These and similar injunctions, made the confused native a little more confused, and it is probable that the battle picture would never have been taken but for certain unforeseen circumstances.

"Now, all men go away, so that there is nobody in sight. And then you shall come from here, and you from there, and fight, and when I run to you and say 'Stop' you shall all lay down your spears."

At the moment the actors withdrew, ready for the mimic battle, Obaga came swiftly along the forest path, and with him his brother and his ten kinsmen and their kinsmen by marriage.

"Man, where is my woman?" said Obaga, and he addressed the tall lover of M'Libi.

"Who knows, hunter?" replied the man.

"You know now, but how long will you know?" said Obaga, and struck with his spear.

His enemy twisted slightly, took the cut across his shoulder and ran. Obaga's spear brought him to the ground. And in a second there was war.

Into the open they came, cutting, parrying, thrusting, yelling those shrill cries, meaningless but ominous, which the Ochori have screamed throughout ages.

"Stick it!" yelled Bones. "Turn the handle, Ahmet. That's good! Go it, boys!" he shrieked in his best producer's style. "That's it, a little more to the left. Don't hurt yourselves, you silly old jossers!"

And then in Bomongo he roared! – "I come."

He strode with a dignified and picturesque swing of his shoulders into their midst, and raised his hand in a lordly gesture.

"Stop!" he cried. But they did not stop. A spear knocked his helmet off, a war club brought him to his knees. Bones reached for his gun, but he had not come armed. Fortunately, Sergeant Ahmet had...

"I thought it was a bit too realistic," explained Bones, who had spent the morning admiring his bandaged head in a looking-glass. "But, of course, I never dreamt that there was a jolly old war on. And when you come to think of it, dear old Ham, it wasn't half a bad stunt – my being knocked out. It'll look so wonderfully thrillin' that people will just sit tight in their jolly old seats and howl! I'll bet it's in all the papers, dear old Ham," he went on. "The jolly old *Times*, and the dear old What-you-may-call-'em – "

Bones spent the night in a dark and smelly hut, illuminated only by a faint red glow from his developing lamp. But though he covered himself from head to foot in hypo, though he dipped and dipped the film until his arm ached, and conformed faithfully to every law contained in the book of instructions, he produced nothing but a succession of little black oblong blobs.

"Most extrordinary, dear old boy," he said miserably. "Most amazing! Can't understand it, dear old thing. There's a fortune gone west, ab-so-lutely west!"

"Who turned the handle?"

"Ahmet. I taught him, dear old Ham. Taught him, and he did what I told him to do. That's the horribly hideous part of it."

For all his faith in Ahmet, he interviewed that gentleman.

"You didn't open the little door, of course, Ahmet? The-door-that-must-never-be-opened?" he asked solemnly.

"Lord, I opened it, but only for a little time, whilst I looked for some pictures which I had improperly taken, without your lordship's knowledge. But they were not there."

"In daylight did you open it?" asked Bones in horror.

"No, lord, in sunlight," said Ahmet, "but there was nothing there, as I have told your lordship, only a yellow ribbon and no pictures!"

THE HEALER

Men lie with a certain transparent simplicity in the lands that border the Great River. Their falsehoods are easily detected, and are less falsehoods than inventions, being so elaborated and painted in such primitive colours that no man is deceived.

For they lie as children lie, about remarkable things and happenings that could not be: such as two-headed dogs that spit smoke, and trees that walk about, and little bees that fall in love with beautiful maidens. If they lie for safety or business purposes, they do so haltingly or sullenly, as the circumstances command, and are to be brought to the frank truth with a sharp word.

Such a liar as Lujaga, the petty chief of the Inner N'gombi, was a rarity, and he was one of three men who, in twenty years, completely deceived Mr Commissioner Sanders.

And talking of liars...

"There's a lot about you, Bones," said Hamilton, "that reminds me of the Isisi."

"Dear old officer," murmured Bones reproachfully, "why compare a jolly old comrade to the indigenous native?"

"I was thinking more particularly of your interesting contribution to the *Guildford Times*," said Hamilton.

He was sitting on the verandah after tiffin, smoking a lazy cigar, and as he stretched out his arm, he picked up from the floor a newspaper that had come by the mail. Bones glanced at the title and shuffled his big feet uncomfortably.

"Dear old officer," he pleaded, "if you're going to spring on me a little flight of fancy, a jolly old *jeu d'esprit*, so to speak – "

"I have been reading your account of how you chased the wild okapi through the forest," said Hamilton relentlessly, "and how, when it was at bay, it turned and snarled at you. The okapi doesn't live in this country anyway, and if he did he wouldn't snarl. He would neigh or he would bray. Possibly he would bray, recognising you as a man and a brother, but he would not snarl or, as you suggest, show his fangs. He hasn't any fangs to show, though I dare say he could pick up a few in his travels if he had the mind of a collector."

Sanders strolled out at that moment and stood, an interested listener, in the doorway.

"Listen to this," said Hamilton.

"Dear old Ham," begged the agitated Bones, "why pursue the jolly old subject?"

"Listen to this," said the remorseless Hamilton.

" 'As the okapi swung round and faced me I reached for my rifle! It was not there! My terrified native bearer had bolted! I was alone in the jungle with a fierce okapi! He leapt at my throat! I dodged him! In that moment all my past life swam before my eyes! Whipping out my revolver, I fired at him twice! He fell lifeless at my feet!' "

Hamilton glared over the top of the paper. "Liar!" he said simply.

"Dear old sceptical superior," said Bones, speaking with a certain dignity, "you seem to forget the colourless lives that the jolly old Guildfordians live. As a matter of fact, they wrote and asked me to give them a little story of adventure for their Christmas number."

"That makes it more understandable," said Hamilton. "You tried to write a fairy story. Well, you succeeded. But you're showing up the service, Bones. An officer in these territories ought at least to know that the okapi is something between a donkey and a zebra, and that he wouldn't show fight even to a mouse."

He picked up another newspaper.

"Who sends you these infernal things?" asked Bones irritably. "Bless my jolly old life," he added a little incoherently, "is there nothing sacred, nothing private? Can't a fellow – "

"There's nothing sacred about the twopence I paid for this newspaper," said Hamilton. He opened the pages with exasperating leisure, and Bones writhed. "Here is the second part of the serial. I won't read it all. It is headed" – he glanced at the top of the column – "A Fight with Vampires."

"Don't let's have any unpleasantness," said Bones, but Hamilton was not to be denied.

"This is the bit I like best?

" 'At night I was awakened – '

"By the way, they've corrected your spelling, I observe –

" ' – by a shrill, whistling sound and a sense of keen pain in my toe. Looking up, I saw a huge, shadowy shape floating at the foot of my bed. It was a vampire! Not daring to move, I watched, fascinated, the hideous animal – ' "

"I should have said 'bird,' " murmured Bones, "or perhaps 'reptile'."

"Or 'fish'," suggested Hamilton. "But don't interrupt.

" 'Its baleful eyes were fixed on me like two green moons! I reached out my hand stealthily – ' "

"I hope they've only put two l's in 'stealthily,' " said Bones with a cough.

" 'I reached out my hand stealthily,' " Hamilton went on, ' " and seized a pistol that lay on the bedside table! It was not loaded! What should I do? With all my strength I hurled myself upon the dreadful insect – ' "

It was Sanders' long chuckle of delight which interrupted the reading.

"Bones, you're really wonderful," he said, as he came forward and pulled up a chair. "I presume it was our visit to the Isle of Bats which inspired that classic."

In the Middle River, four days' steaming from headquarters, is a long island where the bats live by day, hanging in huge clusters, not by the thousand but by the million; and Bones and he had spent an eerie evening watching these things of the night wake to life.

"The question is," said Hamilton as he folded the paper, "is or is not a man who writes that kind of stuff a natural liar; and has or has not Bones the Isisi mind?"

"The Isisi mind is the mind of a poet, Bones," said Sanders, "and if I were you I'd plead guilty. Whilst on the subject of gay deceivers, may I mention that I shall want you to go up into the Inner N'gombi tomorrow perhaps – perhaps not for a week or so? There is a brand new cult come into being, and one Bobolara is its prophet."

Hamilton looked up quickly. "Leopards?"

Sanders shook his head. "Not Leopards this time. It is something with a little witch doctorery in it, and I want it checked before it goes any farther. A healer of healers is amongst us, and he has made his appearance, of all places in the world, in the Inner N'gombi."

There was a time when the Inner N'gombi were a thorn in the flesh of administration. Loyal to none, responsible only to themselves, they took toll of their neighbours with freedom and violence. There had been a hanging or two, a few beatings, a chief deposed to the Village of Irons, a headman hunted into the bush, a village or two burnt, before Lujaga, son of Lofuru, had been elevated to the chieftain's rank, and thereafter all trouble had ceased. It is true that his neighbours complained of midnight raids upon their property; a few women had disappeared from the Ochori; and Bosambo had carried his spears to the border. But Lujaga, summoned to palaver, had given a very frank explanation.

"Lord," he said, "my people are a haughty and warlike people, who have never been yoked. And there are little chiefs who call me king in a small voice, and call themselves master loudly. The Ochori women were taken by a small chief, who carried them into the forest. My young men are at this moment trailing him."

Similarly, when six canoes of the Upper Isisi had vanished *en route* to headquarters, carrying the rubber which formed their contribution to the revenue, Lujaga had been quick to detect the culprits. He came personally to the end of the river with more than half of the stolen property.

"I bring no heads," he said significantly, "for it is your will, Sandi, that there shall be no killing. But when thieves fight for spears, shall we clap our hands and laugh? There are bad men in the forest by the river, and these went out and held up the Isisi canoes, killing the paddlers. Now, what is your will?"

Proof after proof of Lujaga's honesty came to Sanders. Once, the first news of a raid on the Isisi came from Lujaga himself and with it two men captured by the king's soldiers – silent, pained men, who did not speak because their tongues had been cut out, a fault to which Lujaga had frankly confessed.

"Fighting men have their ways, lord," he said. "I cannot hold my young men in the heat of battle, for they are savages, but the men who did this have been whipped and burnt."

He paid his taxes regularly; his villages that fringed the river – for, though his territory in the main lay in the inner forest, it extended to the banks of the water – were models of order and cleanliness. His spies brought invaluable news from the frontier, and he made no complaints against his neighbours.

"Lujaga is a model chief," said Sanders, not once but many times, and he showed him certain favours, such as remitting portions of his taxation and giving to him hunting rights within the no-man's-land that ran to the borders of the French terrritory.

Only one man had ever attempted to undermine Sanders' faith in the chief and that man was Bosambo, king of the Ochori. Bosambo trusted few and respected nobody. One day he came to the headquarters with a long story of raids, of forest rights violated, of women and goats that had disappeared from a frontier village, and

Sanders listened patiently, putting in his discounts at various stages of the narrative, and in the end, gave judgment.

"News of this shall go to the Lujaga," he said. "The chief will find the men who did this, and your women and goats shall come back to you."

"All?" said the sceptical Bosambo. "Lord, I do not doubt that Lujaga will return one woman in three and one goat in six, for that is his way. All the rest you will find in the compounds of his secret city. For this man is a liar."

"Who is not?" asked Sanders, and there the palaver ended.

They called the city of the king "secret" because it was tucked away in the heart of a dense wood twelve hours from running water, and therefore hard to come by. In his secret city lived Bobolara, the Healer, one who was known beyond the confines of his own territory. He was a tall man of singular beauty and character, and as a child he had performed many miracles, for he had rubbed sick men on the back and they had recovered; and he had taken away terrible headaches by twisting the neck of the sufferer in a peculiar and mysterious way. When a tree fell upon a woodman and put out his shoulder, and a palaver of the village elders had condemned the man to death, because the misshapen are never tolerated, Bobolara had by his magic twisted the shoulder back into its place, so that in a week the woodman was about his business again.

He lived in a little hut at the far end of the main village street, and was accounted peculiar in that he had neither wife nor love affair. When he walked past the huts on an evening, he glanced neither to the right nor to the left, and no married woman turned her guilty eyes upon him.

The king Lujaga knew him by name, and one turbulent and stormy night had sent a messenger to his hut, bidding him come. Bobolara came to the king's great hut, and beheld a girl lying on the floor of the hut, moaning her terror, half mad with fright and bleeding from a wound in the back.

"This woman I took from an Ochori hut," said Lujaga, "and one of my soldiers speared her. I have given him to death, but this woman must be saved, for she is very beautiful and I desire her for my house. Now, take her to your hut, Bobolara, and by your magic heal her, and in three and three days bring her to me full of love and in some respects as she is today."

Bobolara had the girl carried to his hut and tended her wound, and in three days she had recovered her sanity, and Bobolara had learnt to pity which in all peoples is half way to love. On the sixth day the king sent his familiar, a small man called Ligi, to bring his bride to the great feast which he had prepared in the centre of the city. Here, before his hut, he had assembled his dancing girls and his warriors for the ceremony of betrothal. But Bobolara came alone.

"Where is the woman?" asked Lujaga.

"She is with her people," said Bobolara calmly. "For, king, this woman does not belong to us, and I have set her free. I guided her myself through the forest by night."

It was some time before Lujaga recovered from shock, and then he struck the man across the face with his whip.

"O dog," he howled, "this night you shall live with ghosts! Take this man to the Little People!"

They seized Bobolara and carried him into the forest near the great anthills, and there they spread-eagled him out on the ground, naked as he was born, and from each anthill was laid a sweet and syrupy trail that would lead the Little People to the prostrate figure. And there they left him for the ants to take him, little by little, until nothing but his bones were left. In the morning, when they came to see what was left, they found him asleep. The ground was black with ants, but none had touched him. So they released Bobolara and brought him back to the king.

"Bend a sapling," snarled Lujaga.

They pulled down a young tree with a rope and tied the free end to the neck of the man.

"Strike," said Lujaga, and the executioner raised his curved knife to strike Bobolara's head from the body.

Before the knife could fall the executioner had stumbled in a fit to the ground, and no one dared take up his knife when the king ordered.

"It is clear to me," said the chief counsellor of the king in a troubled voice, "that Bobolara has a powerful ju-ju. Now, let him go, Lujaga, for I am afraid."

Therefore was Bobolara permitted to live, for the king feared the temper of his people. Nevertheless, two nights later he sent his assassins to the hut of Bobolara.

"Bring back wet spears and I will make you chiefs of villages," he said, but they brought their spears back clean, with the story of a demon that guarded the hut of the Healer, a demon with a blue face and an owl that radiated fire.

For another month the Healer was permitted to continue an untroubled existence. It is said that he raised the dead, but that is probably untrue. He made sick men well; he cured strange sicknesses; he eased women in their terrible pain.

Then a strange thing happened in the secret city. The second counsellor of the king died in pain. Bobolara saw the man and guessed the cause, for the second counsellor of the king was notoriously at enmity with his master.

Bobolara made many solitary journeys into the forest in search of rare herbs, for he had an instinct for beneficial properties. One day, after the death of the king's second counsellor, he saw two men searching at the end of the swamp, where many crocodiles live and strange plants grow that are to be found in no other part of the country. Watching them idly, as they came toward him, bearing in their hands thick branches of a bush speckled red with berries, he recognised Lujaga and his familiar, and at the sight of him Lujaga's face darkened.

"O Healer," he said, "I see you."

"I see you, lord," said Bobolara. "Is the king a doctor that he gathers the little poison berries, that even the great ones of the swamp will not eat?"

"I gather them because they are magical, and keep away spirits and ghosts," said the king glibly.

Bobolara said nothing, and the king hated him more.

Day after day the Healer watched and waited, but no new counsellor was taken with a strange sickness. One night the king spoke secretly to his man.

"Take this message to Sandi at his fine house by the river," he said, and spent the night in giving minute instructions.

Before the dawn, the king's man was on his way with a little bag of white powder hidden in his loincloth...

"I've had a message from Lujaga," said Sanders one morning at breakfast. "This infernal Bobolara is raising the dead! Lujaga is never an alarmist, but he takes a serious view. A number of men and women are disappearing, and he is scared that the Healer is chopping them for medicine."

"I'll give him chop, dear old excellency," said Bones. "I think you can trust me to deal with jolly old birds of that kind. I'll have him back by Wednesday."

"And bring back an okapi," suggested Hamilton, "and be careful he doesn't sting you!"

Bones left headquarters full of energy. With him went Ligi, the king's man, and Ligi served him with food. The day was gloriously fine, the sky an unclouded blue. The vivid green of the spring foliage, the diamond sparkle of the river, the cooling winds that swept down from the mountains a thousand miles away, added to the zest of life.

The next morning Bones did not feel so bright or energetic, although the day was as beautiful and the scene was fair. On the third day there was a curious buzzing in his ears, his eyes were heavy, and two leaden weights seemed pressing on his head. He took ten grains of quinine, and braced himself and cursed all fever-bearing mosquitoes.

He stumbled ashore on the beach of the N'gombi territory, his head throbbing, hearing the far-away voice of the little chief who greeted him, but understanding nothing.

"Lord," said Abiboo, his agitated sergeant, "let us go back to the beautiful ship, and I will take you to Sandi, for you are a sick man."

Bones grinned foolishly. In the twelve-hour march through the forest there was evidence enough that all was not well in the N'gombi country. Every three miles they found a dead man with a curious marking on his chest.

"These Bobolara killed," said Ligi, his guide, "so that he might attain certain power over the people."

Bones nodded stupidly. "This is a hanging palaver," he said thickly, and stumbled on.

One night, in a village ten miles from the secret city, when the fires had been stirred to flame, and men wandered from family group to group, listening here to the stories told a hundred times of old men's valour and young men's gallantry, and the women were chatting pleasantly about sickness, a stranger strode down the twisting path that leads from the forest, and came into the village street, well observed and wondered at. He was tall, broad-shouldered and beautiful to see, for his hair was plastered with clay, and over his shoulder he wore the new skin of a young leopard. A five-feet fighting shield was buckled to his left arm, and in the cunning socket of the shield he carried three light throwing spears, the polished heads of which glittered in the firelight. Also, to his back was strapped a long bow, the wood half covered with monkey-skin. A big hide belt was buckled about his waist, and left and right hung two short, broad-bladed swords. On his face he wore neither the marks of the Isisi, the Akasava, or the N'gombi. Ochori they knew he was not, and he carried himself too finely for a man of the Lower River tribe, who are humble people.

Though a stranger, he seemed to know his way, for he walked unerringly to the hut of the chief of the village, and him he called by name.

"Kofo," he said, "let us talk a little while."

Kofo came blinking from the darkness of his hut and peered across the dancing flames of the fire.

"O man," he said, "who comes to this grand village and speaks to Kofo, who is chief by all rights, and also a man of Lujaga?"

"I am from the city," said the stranger. "Men call me the Healer," and Kofo's jaw dropped, and he stared.

"O ko," he said at last, "that is a bad word for me, for I thought you lived in the king's hut. Now, what do you want of me?"

"A canoe and ten paddlers; also a headman to be in charge. They must carry me through the lakes, for Sandi is on my heels with his soldiers."

Kofo drew a long breath. At that moment a man came running through the village street, and at the sound of the swift patter of his feet Bobolara turned.

"O Bobolara, I see you," said the runner, halting unsteadily before the chief's hut. "Now, a bad thing has happened, for Tibbetti, who is Sanders' son, is dying by poison in the secret city of the king, and they say that you have put magic upon him."

Bobolara looked at the messenger long and thoughtfully, and then: "I go back to the secret city," he said simply, and turned and went back the way he had come, the messenger at his heels.

"Bobolara, if you go back you die," he wailed, for the people of the city loved Bobolara.

Bones lay upon a skin bed before the king's hut, and the dancing flames of the fire showed the white, drawn face of the half-conscious man. Grouped about were a dozen tarboshed soldiers, and in the background a semicircle of curious, peering faces observed the scene with childish interest.

Abiboo was on his knees by the side of the bed, trying to force brandy into the lips of his master, and above all, dominating the scene, the tall figure of Lujaga.

"Now all people see this!" he shouted. "The lord Tibbetti came to take Bobolara, who by his magic has stricken the white man low. Now, you soldiers of Sandi shall find the wicked Healer, and you shall hang him because of his deeds. For Tibbetti is dear to the heart of Sandi – "

So far he got when the interruption came. A man pushed his way through the encircling throng, strode swiftly toward the fire, and, seeing him, the people gasped and the king's eyes narrowed.

"O Bobolara," he said softly, "you have come to death, for these soldiers will kill you because of the magic you have put upon Tibbetti."

"Let them kill," said Bobolara, "but first let me touch the lord."

Abiboo's hand dropped upon the butt of the revolver at his belt, and his brown face puckered with suspicion and anger.

"O man," he said, "for this you shall die!"

But the Healer took no notice, either of the menace or of the gesture. Stooping, he lifted the inanimate figure as though it were a child, and, none barring him, he carried the unconscious Bones through the throng, Abiboo, revolver in hand, following him.

All night long, in the half-darkness of the hut, Bobolara pummelled and massaged, and, squatting in the doorway, Abiboo watched. When the morning light came and the weary Healer looked forth, he saw a tree and from the branch a long rope dangling. He gazed calmly for a while upon the strange sight, and then: "What is that, soldier?"

"When Tibbetti dies, you also die," said Abiboo.

"Then I shall live," said Bobolara with great calmness, "though it will be a night and a night before Tibbetti speaks."

On the third morning, in response to an urgent pigeon-post, came Sanders. He had steamed all night through the shoals of the river and had made a forced march through the forest to the secret city, and, hastily apprised of his coming, Lujaga met him.

"Lord, this is a bad palaver," he said, "for Tibbetti, it seems, fell under the magic spell of the Healer, and now lies sick to death in the man's hut; and because your soldiers are also bewitched by him, they sit outside his door and watch Bobolara working his devils into the belly of my lord."

Sanders gaped at him. "In the hut of Bobolara? What chief are you," he asked with asperity, "that you allow Tibbetti in his hands?"

The king made no reply.

Bones had recovered consciousness that morning, and was being propped up when Sanders stepped, with his catlike tread, into the big hut.

"Hullo, jolly old excellency," said Bones weakly. "Bit of fever, dear old sir. Couldn't find Bobolara: the beggar skipped before I arrived. Dreadfully sorry, but" – he smiled faintly – "I didn't see any okapi either."

"Bad luck, Bones," said Sanders unsmilingly. "So you missed Bobolara. Did he get away?"

"Yes, the beggar got away just before I arrived, but this jolly old doctor's looked after me, and a real good chap he is."

"Oh!" said Sanders. He beckoned the Healer outside. "Speak to me truthfully, Bobolara," he said, "and I will make life easy for you."

He glanced from the man to the dangling rope and smiled inwardly, guessing all that it meant.

"Lord, what shall I say?" said Bobolara. "I am a healing man, cunning in the ways of pain, and knowing the ways of strange poisons, such as the little red berry that grows by the swamp. I have slain none, but I have cured many, and if Lujaga hates me he has his reasons. Lord, I think your son will live."

Sanders inclined his head. "Man, if you speak the truth, another man lies," he said. "Tell me why Lujaga hates you."

Bobolara hesitated. "It was about a woman, lord, who came from the Ochori country. She was brought here in a raid by the king."

"By Lujaga?" said Sanders sharply.

"There are many raids," said the other. "Sometimes women are brought here, sometimes goats. This woman I sent back to her home, which is on the edge of the Ochori, and Lujuga would have killed me, but he was afraid."

"Tell me more of these little red berries," said Sanders.

"Lord, I know nothing of them except that if men eat them they die, becoming very sleepy, with terrible pains in the head."

With a nod Sanders left him and walked slowly through the village street, his head on his breast, his hands gripping his long walking-stick behind him. The king watched him apprehensively, but Sanders passed the hut and came to a halt at the end of the village street. He beckoned a man to him.

"Bring me Ligi, who is the king's man," he said, and they brought Ligi from his hut.

"Ligi, you came with my lord Tibbetti in his fine ship?"

"Yes, master," said Ligi.

"And in a day and a day the sickness came to him," said Sanders, watching the man closely. "Such a sickness as men have who eat the little red berries from the swamp."

Ligi twiddled his bare toes in the dust, a sign of agitation which did not escape the Commissioner. He turned his head and called two of his soldiers.

"Take this man and tie him to a tree," he said simply. "Then you will whip him till he tells all he has to tell."

Ligi did not struggle in the grip of the tall Kano men, nor was he in the mood to be tied to a tree.

"Lord, I am the king's man," he said, "and I did that which he told me to do. Now, I will tell you the truth."

The truth took much telling, and in the end, Sanders sent him on board the *Zaire*, had irons put upon his legs, and then he called Lujaga, the king, to him.

"Lujaga," he said, "you are going a short journey, and I hope the pain will be little."

"I will tell you the truth – " began Lujaga, and Sanders smiled unpleasantly.

"Tell it to the ghosts," he said, and looked meaningly at the tree with the rope.

THE WAZOOS

When Bones brushed his hair, he made preparations beside which the preliminary arrangements of a *prima donna* were feeble and ineffective. Under the broad window of his hut was a dressing-table, on which stood, in serried ranks, row upon row of bottles containing hair tonics of all kinds, cosmetics, fixers, gums, washes and divers other lotions. He had two silver-backed brushes on which his monogram was beautifully engraved, and a wooden brush that would, at any period of its existence, have welcomed a nice hot bath. With this latter, a comb, certain contortions of face, bendings of head, pattings and smoothings, Bones made ready his crown for the day.

He had an especial reason for care one bright day in July, for two days earlier the mail steamer had brought the Hon. Muriel Witherspan; and Bones had fallen in love with her the moment her dainty foot touched the yellow beach.

The Hon. Muriel was the daughter of one Secretary of State and the niece of another. She was an artist, who had conceived the idea of making an exhibition of native studies; and in course of time, preceded by many telegrams, urgent private notes and anxious inquiries from headquarters, she had arrived, to receive a cold, distant and stiffly official welcome from Mr Commissioner Sanders, and the incoherent adoration of Lieut. Tibbetts.

She was pretty and slim and very capable. Bones thought she was the most wonderful woman in the world. She was certainly the most wonderful white woman in the territories, for there was no other.

127

Sanders and Hamilton were at breakfast with their guest when Bones arrived from his toilet. The girl looked up from her plate, surveying the bowing newcomer with a cool and harrowing scrutiny, beginning at his neck (which made Bones very unhappy, for this portion of his anatomy was the constant subject of libel on the part of Hamilton) and ending with his polished locks.

"Good morning, honourable miss," said Bones uncomfortably. "Nothing wrong with my jolly old nut – nothing offensive to your jolly old artistic temperament, my young Academarian?"

"Academician," corrected Hamilton. "Sit down and eat your breakfast, Bones, and shut up!"

"I was thinking how beautiful you looked," said Muriel, and Bones beamed.

"Not really, dear old miss? I was always considered a pretty old baby – 'where have you come from dear old baby out of the nowhere particular into here' – you know the jolly old hymn, honourable young miss? 'Who gave you those twiddly-twiddly eyes of blue, a jolly old angel poked them as I came through.' "

"Good God!" gasped Hamilton under his breath. Bones quoting poetry always had this effect upon him.

"I think you're lovely, Mr Tibbetts," said Muriel with truth, and Bones giggled.

"You're a naughty old flatterer!" he gurgled. "At the same time, Ham, old officer, I've often been mistaken for Henry Ainley. It's a fact, dear old thing. I'm not sure whether it's Henry Ainley or jolly old Owen Nares, but one of those comedians, old thing."

"You're sure you don't mean the performing seals?" asked Hamilton, and Bones closed his eyes in patient resignation.

"I'll take your word, dear old miss," he said. "I don't profess to be beautiful, but I'd pass in a crowd – "

"With a kick," suggested Hamilton.

"And if you want to paint me," Bones went on, contemptuous of the interruption, "well, here I am!"

"And if you'd paint him an invisible blue, so that we couldn't see him," said Hamilton, "you'd be rendering the community and the Government a great service."

"You're very unkind," said Muriel, crumbling her toast, her grey, insolent eyes on Bones. "Mr Tibbetts has the perfect Greek face."

"There you are!" said Bones with a smirk.

"His nose is a little too short for the *perfect* Greek, perhaps, but his chin is rather a dream, don't you think, Captain Hamilton?"

"Have you noticed his cheek?" asked Hamilton sardonically. "That's a nightmare!"

"There's a lot about Bones that is very picturesque — let it go at that," interrupted Sanders with a smile. "He's rather thin, and his habit of stooping is a little unsightly – "

"And his feet are enormous," murmured Hamilton.

"Jealousy, dear old thing, jealousy," said Bones testily. "Don't paint me, dear young honourable miss! I should never hear the last of it."

"Paint him as a curiosity," suggested Hamilton, "and leave a light burning over the picture at night. It would keep the most hardened burglar at bay."

Bones carried off the visitor to give her a few lessons in the art of composition. She had chosen the residency garden and that patch of high gum-trees by the water's edge — a perfect retreat on a hot day.

"If you'll sit over here, dear old miss, you'll see the river and that dinky little village. Isn't that fine?"

"It's perfectly splendid," said the girl. "Put my easel there, Mr Tibbetts, and will you unfasten my stool? And oh, do please go back and get my paints: I've forgotten them."

A dishevelled Bones ran errands for a quarter of an hour, after which the artistic Muriel began to paint.

Stealing forward until he filled the gap between the trees, and, incidentally, in the very centre of her picture, Bones folded his arms, struck a Napoleonic attitude and waited. He waited for half an hour, and when she said: "Do you mind standing on one side, Mr Tibbetts? I can't see the view," he was pardonably annoyed.

Miss Muriel Witherspan, in addition to being a painter, had a passion for information about native life and customs. In one afternoon she exhausted Sanders, in the course of the evening she reduced Hamilton to a nervous wreck.

"Well, it's like this, you see, the Isisi are not exactly the same as the Akasavas.... No, I don't think they have any special customs, y'know – no, they don't eat babies, alive, at least...well, why don't you ask Bones?"

Nothing would give Bones greater happiness, he informed his superior.

"Naturally, dear old duffer, I've studied the jolly old indigenous native more carefully, and – "

"You can lie better, that is all," said Hamilton with asperity. "She wants horrific stories about these innocent people, and you can invent 'em."

"Steady the bluffs, dear old Ham," murmured Bones. "Steady the bluffs!"

"Buffs, you idiot."

"There's only an 'l' of a difference," said Bones, exploding with merriment. "That's rather good, old Ham? Made it up on the spur of the moment, dear old thing – just come out naturally. I must tell dear old honourable miss that!"

"You'll do nothing of the kind," warned Hamilton awfully. "Tell her about human sacrifices."

" 'L' of a difference – that's good enough for *Punch*," murmured Bones, "really awfully good. You said 'Steady the bluffs,' and I said..."

Hamilton left him soaking in the sunshine of his own approval.

The next morning Muriel Witherspan heard of the Wazoos. There was no such tribe on the river, but he had to fasten his stories to some people or other, and she listened open-mouthed.

"Mr Tibbetts was telling me how the Wazoos commit suicide by burying themselves head downward," she said at lunch. And again: "The Wazoos, Mr Tibbetts says, live in trees in summer to keep away from the mosquitoes."

Sanders blinked, but agreed.

To the unfortunate Wazoos, Bones affixed the creations of his fancy. On their behalf he invented a kingdom (he drew it on the firm sand of the beach), and a dynasty beginning with Wog-Wog the First and ending with Boo-Bah the Ninth.

"You've done it, Bones," said Hamilton one morning, meeting his subordinate on the parade ground. "That lady wants to go to Wazooland, and Sanders had to prevent her forcibly from wiring to her lordly parent for permission. It only shows what mischief a ready liar can make."

"I like that!" said Bones indignantly.

"Of course you do – Sanders is taking her up to the Ochori, and is breaking to her gently the fact that the Wazoos *ain't!*"

"Why, you treacherous old officer hound!" protested Bones. "Didn't you tell me – "

"Stand to attention when you speak to your superior officer," said Hamilton sternly.

"Deuced unfair, sir," murmured Bones. "Deuced unsporting, dear old Judas!"

It was Sanders who took her to the Upper River on the *Zaire*, but the chagrin of Bones at being deprived of the privilege of escorting the beautiful visitor was relieved when, the day after the departure of the chief, a pigeon post came to headquarters. Taking the little paper from the pigeon's leg, Hamilton saw that it was from Sanders and marked "Urgent."

"Send Bones instantly to Lujamalababa by *Wiggle*. Arrest and bring to headquarters Saka the witch doctor."

"I suppose you'd better hop," said Hamilton thoughtfully. "That blighter has been seeing things again."

★ ★ ★

In the Akasava country, beyond Lujamalababa, on the farther side of the Great Lake, lived Saka, the sorcerer, who was the son of a sorcerer and the great-grandson of two others. This magic man had power of life and death. He could touch the dead upon their breasts, and they would straightaway open their eyes and speak. And he could look upon a man or woman, and they would disappear and never be seen again. So it was said.

Once, a petty chief and his tribe, who was a very rich man, went away to the Frenchi country to trade skins and ivory, and because he did not trust his relations – as who does? – he left with Saka all his movable wealth, and Saka buried it in his presence beneath the floor of his hut, uttering certain incantations which would produce fatal boils upon the neck of whosoever disturbed the ground; and the small chief went away, satisfied that his riches were safe.

In seven moons he came back and went to the hut of Saka, and they dug up the ground, but no treasure was there.

"O ko," said Saka, in cheerful dismay, "this is because of my magic! For I must have looked too hard at the pretty wonders of yours, M'guru, and they have gone into nothing."

M'guru, who was a trading man and therefore sceptical by nature and training, carried his woes to Sanders, and the Commissioner summoned Saka before him.

"Man," he said, "they tell me you are a great magician, and that whatsoever you look upon disappears. I also am a magician, and lo! I stretch out my hand, and where is the free man who walks without shackles on his legs? He has vanished to my Village of Irons, where bad men labour everlastingly for the Government, and even great chiefs are no higher than fishermen. Now go, Saka, and look well with your wonderful eyes for the treasure of M'guru. And because you are a magician, I think you will find it."

Saka went away, and came back in three days' time with the story of his discovery.

"Lord, by the magic of my eyes I have seen all these wonderful treasures of M'guru. They are buried at three trees by the water, and I have dug them up and given them to M'guru."

"That is good," said Sanders. "Saka, I am a man of few words and many duties. Do not let me come again to this or that palaver, or there will be unhappiness in your hut."

He whiffled his cane suggestively, and Saka, who was an imaginative man, winced. Thereafter, he did much to establish his fame with his people, though all his experiments were not uniformly welcomed. He looked upon the young wife of M'guru, his enemy, and she too disappeared, and M'guru shrewdly suspected that she was not buried near the three trees by the water. He sent for the sorcerer by virtue of his authority.

"Saka, by your magic you shall bring me back my young wife, or I shall bind you for Sanders."

"M'guru," said Saka, surprised, "I did not know that you had a wife; but by my wonderful powers I will find her and bring her to your hut, and you will give me two teeth* because of my talk with the pretty devils who sit around my bed every night and tell me stories."

It happened that Sanders was in the neighbourhood, and the palaver which followed was brief and, to Saka, painful. Thereafter, the sorcerer's eyes ceased to function.

Now, Saka was a sour man of middle age; and, like all witch doctors, intensely vain. The punishment, no less than the loss of his prestige, embittered him; and, being of an inventive turn of mind, he discovered a method of regaining the authority which, whilst it did not profit him greatly, caused intense annoyance to those whom he chose to regard as his enemies. Men and women who came secretly in his hut at night to seek his intervention in their affairs, heard of a new and more potent devil than any that had come to the Lake country. His name was M'lo; he was of microscopic size, and worked his mischief from some familiar article of clothing where he had lodged himself.

"You have fire in your teeth," he said to one supplicant, whose swollen jaw and agonised expression were eloquent of his suffering.

* Teeth = ivory tusks.

"My magic tells me that M'lo is working powerfully against you." He closed his eyes in an ecstasy of divination. "He lives in the blue cloth of E'gera, the wife of M'guru. This you must burn. If you betray me to M'lo, and he knows I have told you, he will kill you?"

The following morning, the beautiful blue cloth which encircled the figure of E'gera, principal and favourite wife of M'guru, vanished, and became a heap of black and smouldering fibre in the recesses of the forest.

To a man whose wife had given him cause for uneasiness (to put the matter mildly) he revealed the presence of M'lo in the growing corn of an enemy's garden, and in the morning no corn stood where the seeker after his hateful oppressor had searched.

He discovered M'lo malignly surveying the village from a fire beyond M'guru's hut, and in the morning it was quenched. And nobody betrayed him because of their fear of the parasitical demon. Nobody save a spy of Sanders, whose business was to know and tell.

He had an interview with Saka, posing as a man who had lost a dog, and Saka told him of M'lo and how the devil might be exorcised by putting fire to M'guru's hut. This he told because the spy was of another village.

Then on a day came Lieutenant Tibbetts with four soldiers, and they carried away Saka the sorcerer to a place where M'lo had no influence.

★　★　★

In the blue dusk which immediately precedes the darkness of night a white steamer picked her way through the pestiferous shoals that infest the river opposite the village of Lugala, and all the people of the village came down to the beach, hopeful that something would occur to afford a subject for gossip during the remaining hours of the night, they being great story-tellers and immensely credulous. Heavy rains had fallen; the shallow bed had silted up; new sandbanks had appeared where deep channels had run before; and the prospect of sensation was not unjustified.

Unconscious of the possibility which heavy rains and shifting sands may bring, the navigator of the steamer came at full speed, a fierce light of resolve in his eye, and the greater half of a banana occupying the cavity of his mouth. In the bow of the *Wiggle* a Kano boy plied a long stick, thrusting it into the water and relating his discoveries in a whining monotone.

"A fathom and half a fathom," he droned, and then: "A fathom."

The *Wiggle* thudded into something soft and, partly yielding, swung broadside to the stream, and stopped.

"Woof...umph...hgg!"

Bones' natural expression of horror and amazement was somewhat distorted by the banana. He swallowed hastily and nearly choked, and then: "O ten and ten fools!" he snapped, glaring down at the perfectly innocent sounding boy. "Did you not say a fathom and a fathom and a half, and here is my fine ship upon the banks!"

"Lord, there is not a fathom and a fathom and a half here," said the sounding boy calmly. "When I spoke we were in such water. Now we are on the sand. It is the will of God."

Bones uttered an impatient tut and looked round. The night had come instantly. From the shore he saw the flicker of fires burning before the villagers' huts, but knew there was no man of the Isisi who would come out to the rescue of the ship, since that implied standing waist-high in a river infested by crocodiles, in order to lift the *Wiggle* to deep water.

He was safe enough until the morning, for the pressure of the current would keep the *Wiggle* fast to the bank. But between safety and comfort was a wide margin. The floor of his sleeping cabin canted over to an angle of thirty degrees. It was impossible either to sit or lie in comfort. Bones ordered out the boat, and had himself rowed to the shore.

That he was expected, he knew before the watch fires began to blaze on the beach. There was a crowd of 500 people waiting to receive him – Lugala had a population of 506 people, but six were too old or ill to journey to the beach. Borobo, the chief, offered him salt and apologies.

"Lord, there are many crocodiles in the river in these days of the year. Yesterday they took a woman from the village of Gobini whilst she was washing her baby on the shore."

"Chief, have no fear. I come with peace in my heart," said Bones magnificently, and stalked up the village street to the guest-house, which was ready for him, the chief having sent secret word that his rare dogs, which were usually kennelled here, should be ejected.

Lieut. Tibbetts' own cook came ashore and prepared him his evening meal, which Bones ate before an audience of 503, three of the infirm and aged being carried out from their huts to witness the amazing spectacle of a man sticking a silver spear in his mouth at irregular intervals.

("It is said," whispered one awe-stricken gossip to another, "that Tibbetti cannot use his fingers because they were bitten by a snake when he was young.")

When, later in the evening, tidings came to Bones that the *Wiggle* had assumed an even more alarming angle, he ordered all men ashore, and Saka was placed under guard in a hut at the end of the village.

Now, Saka's fame was not limited to his own country. He enjoyed, in the regions beyond the frontier of Lujamalababa (or Lugala as it was sometimes called), a reputation which was the envy of many local medicine men, who very properly depreciated his powers. For that is the way of the world, black or white, that small men enhance their reputations by depreciating their betters. And from Bones, the centre of interest, as the night wore on, became, not the hut in which he was lodged and sleeping, noisily, but the larger hut where the philosopher of a foreign people spoke wisdom and initiated the village of Lugala into the mysteries and eccentricities of M'lo, the invisible.

And nobody was more interested than the Houssa sentry who was placed over him, for he was of the Kano people, who believe that his family was under the especial care of a red and green snake, the red half of which was male and the blue half female, and he never went to bed at night without placing a bowl of water near his head, that this especial demon should not grow thirsty.

"Bring to me," boasted Saka, "those who are dead, and I will make them alive, through the wonder of M'lo, who is so small that his village is beneath the foot of an ant! And none can see him save only Saka, who has eyes more wonderful than crocodiles and brighter than leopards. And this little devil of mine is in this village. He sits on the leaf of a tree to make your head ache, O man-with-the-wire-about-your-head; and he sits on the top of a cooking-pot and whispers evil words into the ears of your wives as they boil the fish. But most terrible is he when he dwells in the clothes of white men."

"My daughter has pains in her stomach, Saka," said a man, edging forward. "Also, my garden grows no corn; and monkeys have eaten my wonderful long yellow fruit."

"It is M'lo who has done this," said the other complacently, and screwed up his eyes. "I see him! He is in the white man's clothes. Now, tomorrow morning Tibbetti will go down to the river and wash himself all over, in the manner of these people. Take, then, all of his clothing, also the little silk shirt with hollow legs that he wears in his sleep – these you will find by the shore; and put wood under them and burn them, and I will send M'lo to another village."

"But, Saka, if you do this," said a troubled patient, "he will whip us, being a cruel man. Also, Sandi is within a day's march, and he will come with his soldiers and chastise us, as he did in the days of the war, when he hanged my own father."

"Who shall chastise you most?" demanded Saka, oracularly. "This Sandi, who is only a man, or M'lo, who is a god and a devil and a ju-ju and a ghost, all in one? Who shall save your village from burning, and your young maidens from serious trouble, and your wives from fickleness? Only M'lo, who is so small that he may cook his dinner in the eye of a mosquito, and that terrible bird shall not feel!"

"Lord," said an aged man, shaking his head in fear, "we were a happy people till you came, for we knew nothing of M'lo, having our own devils, as our fathers had."

"To know is to suffer," said Saka, truly and cryptically. "If you will not do these things for me, then you must pass, as many villages have passed. For what did I see on the other bank of the river but a village that was not? And the elephant grass is growing amidst the roof trees, and the graves of the dead – where are they?"

Ten miles up the river was a village in which beri-beri had appeared, wiping out such of the population as would not flee before the scourge.

"Who broke down the walls and rotted the roofs? – M'lo," chanted Saka. "And now he has come here, and I fear you will all die…"

Bones gave an order that he was to be called early. He had hailed with joy the excuse for breaking the journey, for he was most anxious to meet the Hon. Muriel Witherspan on terms that were complimentary to himself, and the *Zaire* was due that day, the chief told him – and he knew, for the *lokali* had been beating the news through the night. Bones, the subordinate of headquarters, was not the Bones in command of an important and special mission. It was only fair that she should know this. She might even find an inspiration in this new view of him.

He imagined the picture of the year at the Royal Academy: a stern, handsome young officer, his sword girt to his waist, his sun helmet pushed back to show the almost Grecian nose and the perfect chin of a born commander. He was standing in the white African sunlight, his hands resting lightly on the barrel of a Hotchkiss gun; in the background, an infuriated mob of indigenous natives, whose bloody spears and blood-curdling yells failed to shake the courage of this cynically smiling young man. (Bones had practised the cynical smile for days.) And the picture would be called, simply: "An Empire Builder," or "The Iron Hand and the Velvet Glove," or something similarly appropriate.

He had neither the time nor the necessary apparatus to do his hair as he would like it to be done, but that was a pleasure in store; Abiboo had brought him the intelligence that the *Wiggle* was free from the sand shoal, and was riding at anchor in the clear waters beyond.

"Take the men on board," said Bones briskly. "We will not sail for an hour or two. I must overhaul the machinery, Abiboo."

Abiboo went and collected his prisoner and men, shipped them on board and sat down to wait. Bones shaved with the greatest care with a safety razor, and, slipping a dressing-gown over his pyjamas, he shuffled down to a secluded cove in the river for his morning bath.

The idea of being depicted in the Academy was an enthralling one. The fact that Miss Muriel Witherspan did not exhibit in the Academy, or anywhere else that made superlative merit a test for exhibition, did not occur to Bones. He saw himself walking before the picture of the year, viewing it with a quiet, quizzical, self-deprecatory smile, and stroll away, followed by turning heads which whispered "That is he! Tibbetts, the Empire Builder."

He was so absorbed with this picture that he stood for some time breast-high in the water, staring solemnly at the *Wiggle* in midstream.

The picture of the year! And why shouldn't she paint it? She seemed a very intelligent young woman, her paint-box was almost new, and must have cost a lot of money. And, anyway, painting was only a question of putting the right colours in the right places.

With a long and ecstatic sigh he turned and swam through the shallow water, and came, pink and dripping, to a patch of grass where he had left his clothing and a towel. But even the towel was gone. His pyjamas, jacket, and trousers had vanished. His slippers, however, he found.

"Hi!" yelled Bones, wrathfully, and the echoed "Hi!" that came back to him from the wood had the quality of derision.

"Goodness gracious heavens alive!" said Bones aghast. He was not three minutes' walk from his hut, but there was no way of reaching that shelter without passing through the village street.

Bones looked round helplessly for leaves, having a vague recollection that somewhere or other he had read of somebody who had formed an extemporised costume from this flimsy material. But the only leaves in view were the smallest leaves of a gum-tree; and Bones remembered he had neither needle nor thread.

"Hi!" he yelled again, purple in the face, but there was no answer.

He turned and looked at the boat. The current was running swiftly, but he was a good swimmer, and –

He saw a swirl of water, the comb of a rugged back, as a crocodile swam down river. It passed, only to turn in a wide circle and swim up again.

"Oh, confound and dash it!" wailed Bones. "Go away, you naughty old crustacean!"

He meant "silurian," but it did not matter.

There was nothing to do but to make a dive for his hut, and he edged cautiously forward down the little path to the village, and presently came within a stone's throw of the nearest hut. A woman passed down to the river with a stone jar on her head. Bones gazed enviously at the grass kilt she wore. Nobody else came into view, and he crept nearer to the hut, and, flattening himself against the rush walls, peeped into the interior. It was empty, and he dashed inside.

But it was not literally empty: stretched on two pegs was one of those identical kilts he had envied − a kilt made of long, pliant grass fixed to a string. And the maker had evidently just completed her labour, for the last strand of grass was not tied. Bones snatched the kilt from the wall and wrapped it round him. It had evidently been intended for a lady of more generous proportions, for the kilt passed twice round his body before it met. There was nothing left but to march up the street. The horrified people of Lugala gathered at the doors of their huts to see the strange and even appalling sight; but Bones, mindful of his dignity, screwed his eyeglass in his eye − thank heaven the unknown robbers had not stolen that − and walked with majesty the length of the street, apparently oblivious to the bewildered or guilty eyes that stared as he passed.

His servant had gone on board the *Wiggle*. His host was not in sight. Bones dived in and began a frantic search for clothes. They also had gone! His bedding had been taken away, his breeches − everything, indeed, except a short silk singlet which seemed, in all the circumstances, inadequate.

Bones put his head out of the door and yelled for the chief, but there was no response. Not that Borobo did not hear him. Indeed, he took trouble to explain to his impressed wives what the commotion was all about.

"The Lord Tibbetti sings every morning, being a young and joyous man. Now listen to his beautiful voice. Such is singing in the way of his people."

"Heavens and Moses!" gasped Bones when no succour came, and he was on the point of stepping out, made shameless by his misfortune, when a familiar sound came to his ear. It was the "honk honk!" of the *Zaire's* siren. Bones sat down and wiped his forehead. Sanders was here! And Hamilton, whom he had dropped at the mouth of the Isisi River to meet Sanders. And the Hon. Muriel! There was a scamper of feet past the door of the hut. All the village was tearing down to the beach to welcome the Commissioner.

Bones waited till he thought the coast was clear, then stepped out of the hut. There was a shriek from the girl attending a cooking-pot before the chief's hut, and he dashed back again. He must be dreaming, he thought; pinched himself – and it was so easy to pinch himself – to make sure, and had very convincing proof that he was awake.

He waited, every second an hour, every minute an eternity, and then there came to him the voice of Sanders.

"That is the chief's hut, Miss Witherspan, and this hut near is the guest-house. You'd better look inside the guest-house: it is less objectionable than the others."

There was a patter of light feet, and Bones screamed: "Keep out, honourable miss! Jolly old Muriel, keep out!"

"Who's that – Bones?" asked Sanders in amazement. "What the dickens are you doing here?"

"Don't come in!" squeaked Bones. "I've got no clothes on."

Incoherently he told his story. There was a sound of suppressed laughter. Of course, Ham would laugh!

"Don't laugh, you silly old ass," said Bones wrathfully. "Go along and get me some clothes, you naughty old captain."

"I had to laugh," said the musical voice of Muriel.

"Good heavens, young miss! Was it you?" stammered Bones.

"It was me. Captain Hamilton has gone down to get you some clothing. Can't I just peep in?"

"No, you can't," said Bones loudly. "Have a sense of decency, dear old artist!"

"Who did this – the Wazoos?"

There was a malignity in her cooing voice that made Bones shiver. Hamilton had told her! The cad!

"Now listen, dear old painter and decorator – " began Bones.

"Mr Tibbetts – you pulled my leg."

"Be decorous!" urged Bones.

"You pulled my leg. I shan't forget it. I'm coming in to sketch you!"

"I've got nothing on," roared Bones, untruthfully, "except a pair of slippers and a kilt!"

Hamilton returned with a mackintosh and a sun helmet, pleading that that was all he could raise. The mackintosh was one which was slightly too short for Sanders. On the lank figure of Bones it had the appearance of a covert coat.

★　★　★

It was three months later before the illustrated newspaper came into the residency; and, opening it idly, Hamilton saw a picture and yelled. It was a black-and-white sketch, which bore in the corner the scrawled signature "MW". It showed Bones in all the glory of singlet and grass kilt, with a sun helmet on his head and an eyeglass in his eye; and beneath was the superscription: "British officer wearing the native costume of the Wazoos."

THE ALL-AFRICANS

The mind of Mr Commissioner Sanders was as two books, the one open for inspection, and, by its very accessibility, defying the suspicion that any other could exist; the second a small tome, bound in steel and fastened with many locks.

Once upon a time Hamilton, skimming his newspapers newly arrived from home, read something and laughed.

"I wish, dear old officer, you wouldn't," said Bones irritably, glaring up from the torture of simple addition. "Just as I was totting up the jolly old pay sheet. I'll have to do it all over again."

"And you'll do it wrong," said Hamilton. "Can't you take that infernal sheet somewhere else, or learn to count to yourself?"

Bones shrugged. "There's only one way, dear old Ham, and that's the right way," he said, and began his labours anew. "Eight and four's fourteen," he muttered fiercely, "and nine's twenty-two and three's twenty-five and nine's thirty-two an' seven's thirty, one, two, three, four…"

"What were you laughing at?" asked Sanders, smoking a meditative cheroot, his eyes on the parade ground.

"Something in one of the papers about an All-Africa Empire, with an army of its own, organised by American negroes and having their Inspector-General — where do they get such rot from?"

"And nine's a hundred and five, and six is a hundred and ten and three's ninety-nine…" struggled Bones.

"It's true."

Hamilton sat up. "What…? But not here…in the territory?"

143

Sanders nodded. "I've known about it for three years," he said with surprising calm, "and of course it is inevitable. Clever and rich American negroes were certain to exploit Africa sooner or later."

Bones had dropped his accountancy, and was listening open-mouthed.

"You don't mean to tell *me*, sir an' excellency, that the jolly old indigenous native is organisin' a – a...?"

"I mean even to tell you," said Sanders with a smile. "There's a French boat calling next week with a man named Garfield on board and a lady etymologist from England. She wants to go up country to hunt butterflies, and I'm rather worried about the lady."

It seemed that Sanders was changing the subject, but that impression was to be corrected.

"Bones and I will leave tonight," he said, surprisingly, "and you will send me on the letter she brings – open and decode it, and fly me a pigeon with the gist of it. By the way, she is rather pretty, which makes me just a little scared. Yes, the African Empire movement is a reality – I wish it wasn't. Look at Mr Garfield's hands, by the way, particularly his fingernails. He has the permission of Downing Street to explore the country – hoof him along and tell him I'm tax-collecting."

He got up and walked out of the room, and the two men stared at one another.

"It may be sun or it may be fever, dear old Ham," said Bones solemnly. "And yet he must be right in his head – he's taking me along with him."

"It is incredible," said Hamilton, too perturbed to be offensive. "And yet, when Sanders talks and looks like that... You lucky young devil!"

The *Zaire* left at sunset, which was unusual, for the river is full of shoals and navigation a danger. By night (the third night) Sanders brought his steamer to a creek near the village of Kafu...

And then a whisper ran through the village, a whisper that had a gasp at the end, and at that whisper even old men slapped their lean thighs as at the prospect of tribulation, and said in dismay, "Ok'ok'ok'ok a!" which is misery's own superlative on the big river.

For a malign miracle had happened, and there had materialised, under their very eyes, in shape to be seen and in substance which daring men might feel, the most horrific of the river legends.

Sandi-by-night had come, and Sandi-by-night was a distinct and deadly personality. He had arrived from nowhere between sunset and moonrise, and now sat before the hut of Molaka the fisherman. Bold men, peering fearfully from their little houses, saw him, a stooping figure in a grey-green suit, which in the flooding moonlight seemed to possess a radiance of its own. His face was in darkness, for the brim of his big helmet threw a black shadow, and, moreover, his back was toward the serene orb that touched the fronds of the palms with a silver edging.

Whence he came none knew or troubled to think. For Sandi was well known to possess magical qualities, so that he could fly through the air or skim on his feet across the water at an incredible speed.

And he had come, not to the chief's hut, but to the humble dwelling of this eloquent fisherman, who told such beautiful stories.

Sandi was talking in liquid Bomongo. "Also it seems you have spoken to the people of the Forest, Molaka."

"Lord, they like my pretty stories," pleaded the man; "and because I am a poor spearer of fish and desire to please all people, I tell them tales, though I am often weary."

Sanders chuckled softly. "What race are you, Molaka, for I see that you have no cuts on your face such as the people of the Middle River make upon their children?"

"I am from the Lapori River near Bongunda," replied Molaka.

Again he laughed, this slim figure that crouched on the stool which Molaka had brought for him.

"*O Bantu*, you lie!" he said, and then he spoke in English. "Your name is Meredith; you are a native of Kingston, Jamaica, and you are a general in the All-Africa Army."

There was a silence.

"You are one of five hundred specialists especially trained by the Black Africa Syndicate to organise native rebellion," Sanders went on in an almost monotonous tone. "My men have been watching you for two years! You were trained at Louisville College for coloured men for this job, and you receive two hundred dollars a month for your services."

"*Sic itur ad astra,*" Molaka quoted with a certain smugness.

"It is indeed the way to immortality," said Sanders grimly. "Now, tell me, my man, when did you last see a Supreme Councillor of your pestiferous order?"

Molaka yawned ostentatiously. "I'm afraid I cannot afford you any information, Mistah – er – I haven't the honour of knowing your name. I suppose you are Sanders, that these dam' niggers talk about?" (He himself was as black as the ace of spades, though his English was excellent.) "So far I have had the luck to miss you."

Sanders said nothing, then: "When did you see one of your bosses last?"

"I can give you no information," said Molaka, or Meredith, rising. "I presume you will deport me? I shall not be sorry. I have spent two miserable years in this wilderness, and I shall be glad to go home to my dear home town."

Sanders rose too, and now he towered above the squatting figure.

"Come," he said, and strode through the village behind his prisoner.

The people saw them pass, and tapped their teeth in terror. The two men vanished into the forest path. At two o'clock in the morning, the village watchman, dozing over his fire, heard a shriek and leapt up. The cry was not repeated, and he went to sleep again.

In the morning they found a place, just outside the village, where a man had evidently been pegged, spread-eagle fashion, to the ground, for the thongs that had bound his ankles and wrists were still attached to the peg. Also, there were the ashes of a fire and a piece of iron which had been heated. From these indications, the men of the village concluded that Molaka had been asked questions.

It is certain that he did not tell Sanders of the great palaver which was to be held in the country south of the Isisi River, because the messenger who brought him a summons to the *likambo* arrived after he had disappeared – whither, no man ever knew, though the slaves who toil for Government in the Village of Irons might have given information. As to the palaver and its venue, Sanders was to make discovery in another way.

★ ★ ★

There was a man who lived in the country behind Bolibi, who was very wealthy. He ate dog every day of his life, and his wives occupied seventeen different huts. Therefore they called him "Jomo-Nsambo," which means "ten and seven." His plantations of corn and manico covered the land in patches, and in these his wives worked constantly. He was a just man and used the *chicotte* with great discernment, never beating even a woman unless she had committed a foolish act.

One day he went hunting with his young men, for, although he was neither chief by choice nor Government-appointed *capita*, he exercised a lordship even over chiefs, by reason of his wealth, and crooked his finger for all the following he needed.

Whilst he was in the forest, his tenth wife, N'kama, received a lover near the Pool of the Skies, which is a dry pan in the summer and a marsh in the rainy season, and for this reason is so called.

The lover was a tall young man and a greatly popular man with women. Yet because he loved the tenth wife of Jomo-Nsambo, he was faithful to her for one season. His name was Lolango, which in the Bomongo language is "The Desired."

"Woman, I have slept seven nights in this forest waiting for you," he said, "and it is very good to touch you. For two moons I have wanted you, as you know, for was I not a guest in your husband's hut, and did I not say exciting things to you when he slept? But you have been as cold as a dead fish, though I have sent you wonderful words by the woman Msaro who is your servant."

"Lord," she said meekly, "I could not believe that the Desired would desire. And all the stories Msaro told me I thought were foolish. Now I am here."

He made love to her in his fashion. The woman was wonderful to him, and he did not wish to leave her, but because there was a secret *likambo*, or council, in the forest by the Kasai River, and that was a two days' journey, he must be parted from her.

"Let me go with you, Lolango," she said, "for I think Msaro hates me, and will speak to my husband when he returns."

But this, in terror of death, Lolango would not do.

"Woman," he said, in a hushed voice, "this likambo is '*Ta* '." And he made a whistling noise to express the awfulness of the occasion, and opened his eyes wide.

The woman heard the forbidden word without displaying any emotion.

"Then I will give you magic to protect you," she said, and he waited two hours whilst she returned to her village and brought back a bag which was filled with little red berries such as are not seen in this country.

"These I bought from a white trader," she said, "and in each lies a very powerful devil called 'The Looker-Behind.' And when you come to the great forest by the Kasai, which, as all men know, is full of ghosts, you shall drop a red berry every time your feet say *bonkama*.* And the red devil shall come out and no ghost shall follow after you."

He shivered, but eyed the handful of berries in his palm with friendliness.

"There are ghosts of great size and ugliness in the forest," he agreed. "Now, I love you for this magic, N'kama, and I will bring back to you a wonderful cloth such as the Jesus women wear to hide their skins."

So he went away, and she looked after him and spat on the ground. Then she bathed her body in the river and walked with swaying hips toward her hut. She had done her part and had no regrets, save for the bag of beautiful red berries. She would gladly have made a necklace of these. But better he took them than that she should tramp two days with him, she thought.

* = one hundred: that is, every hundred paces.

On the outskirts of the village a man met her. He had the Arab features and the Arab litheness of body, but he wore his cloth native fashion.

"N'kama," he said, "where is the man?"

"He has gone, master: also, he has taken the red seeds."

"Tell me, N'kama, is this man Lolango of the river or of the forest people?"

"Lord, he is of the forest," she said without hesitation, "for when he spoke of the secret palaver he made the word 'Likambo.' Now, we folks of the river say 'Jikambo.' "

The man clicked his lips to denote satisfaction, and, putting his hand within the cloth, pulled out a thin, long chain of brass studded with glittering stones.

"This from Sandi," he said, and dropped it into her hand. "Also, if any man or woman speaks evilly of you, you shall say that Sandi breaks men easily."

And he strode away from the ecstatic girl, leaving her open-mouthed and open-eyed at the treasure in her two hands.

A canoe was waiting for the Arab at the water's edge, and four paddlers took him swiftly with the stream. They rounded the bend of the river and set the canoe's nose toward what appeared to be an impenetrable barrier of tall elephant grass.

There was a passage, however, wide enough for their ingress, and even wider, for on the far side of the screening grass was the *Zaire*, on the bow of which Sanders sat smoking.

He turned his head as the Arab came aboard. "Hullo, Bones!" he greeted the "Arab" in English. "Has the woman gone with Lolango?"

"No, but he has taken the jolly old beans."

Sanders nodded and frowned. "Bones, I don't like things," he said. "I have never known the people to be so uncommunicative. Usually, even over a ju-ju palaver you could find a fellow who was willing to open his mouth. But these devils are dumb."

He stood up suddenly as the "toot-toot" of a steamer siren came from the river. It was the little flat-bottomed French coasting steamer that occasionally penetrated the river as far as the rapids. Standing on the whale deck of the boat so that he could see across the tops of the grasses, he focused a pair of prismatics to his eyes.

"That's the French steamer, and unless I am greatly mistaken, that is our friend Garfield and the lady etymologist on the after deck."

"What is she doing in this country?" asked Bones, puzzled.

"What are women doing anywhere?" demanded Sanders savagely. Then he turned to the pipe-smoking Arab. "So Lolanga has gone?" he said. "And the woman – ?"

Bones spread out his hands.

"It is an unwholesome business," said Sanders, with a grimace of disgust.

Bones puffed noisily. "My dear old excellency," he said, "she's a wicked lady, and she's got millions of naughty old boys anyway."

"I suppose it is all right," said Sanders, "but I hate the thought of women being employed to trap men."

"It isn't an employment, dear old sir," said the cynical Bones, "it is a recreation."

And then, raising his eyes, he saw a pigeon circling and heard the excited calls of the grey birds housed in the coop above the deck cabin.

"Your bird, I think, sir," he said, and whistled the pigeon down.

★ ★ ★

The steamer which carried Miss Honor Brent and her companion stopped at the village of Bofuru, which is not a regular landing-place.

Mr Garfield was a man of fifty. He had a square, white face, and stiff, upstanding hair, and it was he who had suggested the landing. The girl who landed with him was past her first youth, but pretty, and there was in her voice and movement a suggestion of capability which had puzzled her companion, for they had been fellow-passengers from London to Sierra Leone. Bofuru might be an interesting centre, for her object in coming to the Congo (she had said) was to add to her collection of butterflies. Curiously enough, Garfield had anticipated her acquiescence.

"It is a wonderful part of the river for butterflies," he said. "I've seen them ten inches across from wing to wing."

"You know the country, then?"

"I've been here three or four times," he said, carelessly. "I am interested in the palm-oil industry."

They landed on the slip of beach at a time when the village of Bofuru was all agog with awful wonder.

For days strange men had come down the river in their canoes, had landed here, leaving their craft high and dry on the beach, and the villagers had watched them in awestricken silence. For was not "*Ta*" abroad? and had not secret word run from hut to hut that the Great Ones of the land would pass through Bofuru on their way to a *jikambo* (it is true they use the "j" on the river) of ultra-magnificence?

The visitors came generally between dawn and the sun-on-the-trees, because there was a Government post to pass, and the very furtiveness and secrecy of their arrival gave them additional importance. There were solitary paddlers and delegates who came in larger canoes with their own paddle-men, there were chiefs, great and small, known and unknown, and they went into the forest, and the forest swallowed them up.

The advent of two white visitors was the culminating moment of an exciting two days. The villagers stood with folded arms and incredulous faces, watching the landing, until Mr Garfield beckoned his finger at the man who appeared, by reason of the medal hung upon his breast, to be chief.

"*O Bantu*," he said, "prepare a hut for this lady, who stays a while, for she is a very clever woman who seeks flowers-with-wings."

"Lord, she shall have the hut of my wife's own sister," said the chief, "and if she is a God woman, I will send all my people to listen to her beautiful words."

"This is no God woman," said Garfield, and his Bomongo was perfect. "Now keep her and guard her, and do not let her stray into the forest, which, as you know, is full of devils."

He explained to the girl what arrangements he had made for her. Six strange carriers had come from the interior to carry his luggage – strange to the people of Bofuru.

They headed their burdens and marched away with that curious, springing pace which is the natives' own.

"Perhaps you will walk to the edge of the village with me?" said Garfield, and she assented.

They talked of things and of people, neither of any great importance, until they reached the thick bush out of sight of the village. Here the path turned abruptly through a forest of great topal trees.

"I think I'll say good-bye," said the girl with a smile. "I am going to see my hut. You will be returning in four days, you say, Mr Garfield?"

"I shall be returning in four days," repeated Garfield, and looked at her strangely.

A hint of her danger came to her, but she did not change colour, and not a muscle of her face moved as she held out her hand.

"I think not," said Mr Garfield, and his big hand closed on her arm. "You will continue the journey, Miss Brent. I don't know whether that is your real name, but I am not curious. Your hut has been prepared for you, and if you do not go back the natives will understand, for this forest is full of treacherous marshes."

"What do you mean?" she asked, and now she was as white as death.

"I was warned before I left New York that an agent of the British secret service would come on board at Plymouth," he said, speaking slowly, "and that that agent would probably be a woman. Any doubt I had upon the matter was removed when I searched your cabin on the night of a dance we had just outside Madeira. Your instructions were to get into my confidence and accompany me so far as it was safe for you to do so. You have gone just beyond that point." He smiled, and it was the first time she had seen him smile.

"Now, Miss Brent, as you have been instructed to watch the Inspector-General of the All-Africa Army, I am going to bestow upon you the privilege of being present at a council of war. If you scream I shall strangle you until you are silent, and then I shall hand you over to my carriers."

She was breathing quickly. "How absurd you are!" she said bravely. "This is a little comedy of yours – "

"A little tragedy, I think," he corrected her.

He took her arm and, realising the futility of resistance, she went with him.

"We have not far to go, though our rendezvous will be a difficult one for our friend Sanders to find."

"I have no friend – I have never seen Mr Sanders," she said, and he chuckled.

"You will be a little more talkative later on," he said significantly. "Mr Sanders, by all accounts, does not hesitate to employ coercive methods when he is anxious to discover something from an unfortunate agent of ours who falls into his hands."

"I tell you I don't know him," she cried, for the horror of her situation was dawning upon her. "I swear I have never met him, and that I have no knowledge of his existence."

"That we shall discover," said Garfield again.

They trudged along for some time in silence, leaving the beaten path and following a native guide through the trees.

The unmarked way was an extraordinarily tortuous one, and the girl understood why, when now and again she glimpsed the waters of a great swamp. Every two hours they rested, and at the second rest the man gave her chocolate and water from the big skin which hung from the guide's shoulder.

"What are you going to do with me?" she asked, putting into words the thought which had occupied her mind all day.

"After?" For the second time he smiled. "You will not give information to your friend Sanders, that I promise you," he said significantly.

"You're going to kill me?" she asked wildly, starting up.

"Nothing so unpleasant," he said, and offered no other information.

They came at last to the strangest village she had ever seen. A circle of new huts evidently built for this convention. The place was alive with men – she saw no women – who looked at her in wonder as she passed, but saluted Mr Garfield with every evidence of respect and fear.

They were met outside the village by a young native, who spoke English until, with a sharp word, Garfield silenced him. She was conducted to a hut, and a native squatted in front of the door to prevent her escape, and there she sat until the night came and the big moon showed through the tracery of the trees. She heard movements and caught the reflection of a great fire which burnt before a newly erected palaver-house, and now and again she heard the sing-song of a man crying "Kwa!" which meant "Silence!" and another voice speaking in the Bomongo dialect, which she recognised as Garfield's.

And then they brought her out. The pleasant Mr Garfield she had known was not the man who sat on a carved stool under the thatched roof of the palaver-house. Except for a cloth wound about his waist, the loose ends of which were sewn up over his shoulder, he was as innocent of clothing as any of his audience. A strange, obscene figure he made, with his dead-white skin and his bristling black hair, and the incongruity of his appearance was heightened by the fact that he wore his black-rimmed spectacles.

At another time she could have laughed, but now she was speechless with fear.

"Brent." He spoke in English and addressed her by her surname. "My brethren desire that you should speak and tell them of Sanders and the letter you handed secretly to the English officer at the mouth of the river."

She looked round at the scowling faces and past them, in the direction, as she guessed, of Bofuru, and he read her thoughts.

"There is no escape for you," he said. "Get that out of your mind, my friend. No human being could find his way across the marsh even if friend Sanders was on hand. Now, you shall tell me" – his manner changed suddenly, and his voice was harsh – "where is Sanders?"

"I do not know," she said, and her voice was husky.

"Then I will find a way of making you speak," he answered through his teeth, "as Sanders made Molaka speak. What was that letter – you know its contents?"

There was no spoken answer. Only there ran through the squatting figures a man who crouched, a man in grey-green uniform suit, who came swiftly yet stealthily, a long-barrelled revolver in each hand.

He came from nowhere, but, looking past him with staring eyes, Garfield saw the glitter of bayonets, and in the light of the fire, the red fezes of Government soldiers, and dropped his hand to where, concealed by his waistcloth, his pistol belt was strapped.

Sanders fired twice, once from each hand, and the square-faced man stood suddenly erect, covering his face with those tell-tale hands of his – the hands with the half-moon nails that betrayed his native origin. Then he as suddenly fell, and there was no life in him when Sanders turned him over.

★ ★ ★

"You who are chiefs shall be chiefs no longer," said Sanders, sitting in the palaver-house an hour later, and addressing a confused and miserable assembly. "This is the order of the Government. As to the young man who is a foreigner amongst you and speaks English and teaches you cunning ways of fighting, he shall hang before you all. This, too, is the word of my lords." He paused a moment. "Come to me, Lolango."

The tall native who was called "The Desired" came forward in trepidation.

"O Lolango," mocked Sanders, "because you put upon the ground red berries which have a great magic, you are pardoned."

"Lord, I did this because of a woman," stammered Lolango.

"That I know," replied Sanders grimly, and well he knew it, for it was by those red berries dropped at intervals that he had found his way across the swamp.

He turned to the white-faced girl by his side. "I think, Miss Brent, that this is no job for you. I have decided views about the employment of women for Secret Service work."

"I didn't expect I should have to come so far," said the girl ruefully. "I – I did my best to make him talk on the ship, but he was very reticent."

"Now he is more reticent than ever," said Sanders.

THE WOMAN WHO SPOKE TO BIRDS

There was a man named Pinto Fernandez who was called, by courtesy and right, "Portuguese." He possessed an indubitable title to that description, for he was born a native of Angola, being the consequence of a union between a minor official of Sao Paul de Loanda and the half-coloured maid to the wife of His Excellency the Governor of Bonguella. Even by Portuguese standards, Pinto was "dark." It is not necessary to trace his career from Loanda to Sierra Leone, nor to mention more than this fact, that he took a school certificate at one of Marriott Brothers' educational establishments.

His wife was indubitably white. She had been a Miss Hermione de Vere-Biddiford, and at one time was partner to Professor Zoobola, the famous hypnotist and illusionist, who "travelled" the coast from Dakfur to Cape Town. She spoke with a strong Cockney accent, and her father's name was Juggs, so that the balance of probability is weighted toward the supposition that Vere-Biddiford was a nom-de-guerre adopted to meet the exigencies of a profession which demands classiness.

Pinto knew the coast backwards. Before he met his wife, left derelict at Grand Bassam by a bankrupt professor, he had served terms of imprisonment in French, German, Portuguese, and British West African gaols, for divers petty larcenies, impersonations, and trickeries. His wife, on the other hand, had only twice appeared before a magistrate, on each occasion charged with attempting to obtain money by threats.

Mr and Mrs Pinto Fernandez met in the waiting-room of the magistrate's court at Lagos, and were expelled from the country together. At Funchal, in the island of Madeira, they were legally married, and rented a small house in one of those steep streets down which it is the delight of the visiting tourist to toboggan. And there, combining their separate understandings of the people and atmosphere of the coast, and aided largely by Pinto's command of English, they began operations...

Nearly twelve months later: "It seems to me, dear old centurion," said Lieutenant Tibbetts, glaring up from the company clothing accounts, "that either I'm a jolly bad old accountant – "

"I wouldn't say that, Bones," said Hamilton soothingly. "Maybe, as usual, you've added the day of the month and subtracted the year. Or perhaps you've put the pounds in the pence column – try again."

Bones sighed wearily and passed his hand before his eyes. Hamilton could not guess what black despair lay in the heart of his subordinate.

The day was swelteringly hot and the breeze that crawled through the open window of Bones' hut came from landward and had the fragrance and comfort of a large wood fire.

With an effort Bones hunched his shoulders, jabbed the pen into the ink, dropped a large black splodge on his white overalls and began again.

"Nine an' seven's fourteen and eight's twenty-four and three's twenty-five – six, seven, and one's twenty-eight an' four's thirty-six and eight's forty..."

Hamilton did a rapid mental calculation. "The total's right, but the Lord knows how you got it," he said, and reached for the paper.

Suddenly he roared. "You dithering ass, you're adding up the men's chest measurements!"

Bones rose briskly. "That explains the jolly old deficit of eight an' fourpence, sir," he said, and passed the pen. "Audited and found correct – sign!"

"Not on your life, Bones," snapped Hamilton. "Those clothing accounts are a month overdue, and you'll sit down there and make out a new sheet. Sergeant Ahmet complains that you've charged him for a pair of shorts he never had, and there are four shirts, grey, flannel, that do not appear in your account at all."

Bones groaned. "Last week it was brooms, hair, one," he wailed, "and the week before buckets, iron, galvanised, two. Dear old thing, this isn't war! This isn't the jolly old life of adventure that poor old Bones enlisted for! Buckets, dear old thing! What does a jolly old warrior want with a bucket except to kick it, in the glorious execution of his duty, dear old thing?"

Hamilton slid down from the chest of drawers on which he had been sitting and made for the door.

"I'll go into this matter after tiffin," he said ominously. "You are supposed to be stores officer – "

"If there is anything that I'm not supposed to be, dear old Ham," said Bones, with marked patience, "you might mention it, dear old soul. I'm OC Bathrooms and GOC Dustbins, and CIC Chicken-houses. In addition to which, Ham, I'm Inspector-General of Shirts an' Military Controller of Corns – "

"I'll see you after lunch in my official capacity," said his superior. "As a human being, I will give you a long and tingling drink if you will come to my room."

"Barley water?" asked Bones suspiciously.

"Whisky, with aerated water and large and globous chunks of ice."

"Lead me to it, my jolly old Satan," said Bones.

As they were crossing to the residency:

"You really must get out those accounts, Bones," said Hamilton. "I've had a perfectly awful letter from HQ. Besides which, the new half-yearly supply is on its way, and Sanders may want you to go with him into the bush at any minute. And dim the unholy fire in your eyes, Bones – if those accounts are not ready by tomorrow, I will accompany the Commissioner and you can stay."

"Have a heart, dear old fellow creature!" said Bones reproachfully. "I've got quite enough trouble, dear lad. Let me take the accounts with me – "

"If you were going to heaven I wouldn't let you take them," said the firm Hamilton. "And nothing is less likely."

"That I *would* take 'em, dear old cynic?" said Bones. "Maybe you're right, maybe you're right. I'll say 'when,' " he added, as Hamilton uncorked a bottle, "and don't forget, Ham, that drownin' a baby's petty larceny, but drownin' good whisky's a naughty old felony."

It is a fact that Bones had, as he claimed, sufficient trouble. And it was trouble of an unusual kind. It had begun some eight months before, when he had received a letter, delicately scented, and postmarked in Madeira.

"Dear Unknown," it began, and Bones had blushed pleasantly.

It was the story of a young and beautiful woman who had seen him once when the boat on which she was travelling had stopped at the river's mouth to land the mail. She sent her photograph: she told him her life history. She was married to a man forty years her senior. She craved life and youth and freedom. She had for the moment her dreams, and in the very heart of brilliant and soothing visions was "a tall, grave Englishman, whose blue eyes are like flowers in a desert."

Bones spent that day so tall and so grave that Hamilton thought he had a sore throat. He sat up all one rainy night inditing an epistle which was, in a way, a model. It counselled pacience and currage, it embodied sage and fatherly advice, and finished up with all that Bones could remember of a poem which seemed appropriate.

When skys are dark dark and glumy
And every prospecs prospects sad
Look for the jolly old silver linen
For nothings as bad as it seams to be.

It was not good poetry, but the sentiments were sound.

In answer to her second letter (her blessed name was Anita Gonsalez) which came by return of post, Bones was not so fatherly. He was not even brotherly. He was, in fact, skittish. The correspondence proceeded on those lines until there came a black morning in June, and the letter which Bones so eagerly expected did not come. Instead, there arrived a stiff and typewritten document, signed Alfonso Roderique y Trevisa y Gonsalez.

And it demanded the name of Mr Tibbetts' lawyer, and threatened divorce proceedings and social ruin. There were several enclosures and a PS.

"Already the watching of my wife, interception of letters, etc., etc., by first-class detectives has cost me five hundred pounds (English). Am I to let this matter slide and sacrifice expense I have been put to?"

Bones did not reply. Once he was on the point of confiding in Hamilton, but the fear of ridicule (Mr Gonsalez had sent copies of all his letters) made such a confession impossible.

He left a second and a third letter unanswered, and each was more horrific than the last. So that when, that evening, he brought triumphantly a reasonably accurate copy of the clothing account to his chief, and Hamilton, giving it a grudging approval, said: "You're leaving at daybreak, Bones – don't keep the Commissioner waiting as you did the last time," Bones had that sense of overshadowed joy which is experienced by a man respited from a death sentence.

He took Hamilton aside before he went to his hut, and made a request, and the indignant Captain of Houssas all but kicked him.

"Open your letters? Of course I shan't open your letters, you silly ass!"

Bones wriggled in his embarassment and confusion. "The fact of it is, dear old officer…a letter from a lady, dear old sir."

But Hamilton was really annoyed.

A day or two after Sanders and Bones had left, there arrived an intermediate mail-boat which brought little correspondence but a source of considerable trouble.

Hamilton had gone down to the beach to take the mail-bag from one of the ship's officers, when, to his surprise, the life-ship's cutter drove its nose into the soft sand and an elegantly dressed gentleman stepped delicately ashore. One glance told Hamilton both the nationality and the character of the visitor.

"Mr Sanders, I presume?" said Senhor Pinto Fernandez, with an expansive smile on his somewhat unprepossessing face.

He had never worked this part of the coast, and it was his faith that he was unknown in the territory.

"You presume too much, my friend," said Hamilton, eyeing the visitor unfavourably.

"Then you must be Captain Hamilton," said the unabashed Pinto.

He was dressed in the height of European fashion, wearing a tail coat, striped trousers, white spats, and a grey top hat, which in itself was an offence.

"I am Dom Gonsalez from Funchal."

"Then you'd better hurry, for your boat's pulling away," said Hamilton, but, with a graceful wave of his hand, and a smile which was even more genial, Mr Pinto Fernandez conveyed his intention of remaining.

Though Sanders regarded unauthorised visitors as little less than criminals, there was really nothing to prevent any free citizen of almost any nation from landing on the residency beach. And nobody knew this better than Pinto Fernandez.

"The Commissioner is not here, and I am alone on the station," said Hamilton. "If there is any information I can give you, I shall be most happy, but I strongly advise you to keep the boat waiting."

"I am staying," said Pinto Fernandez decisively. "I am here on a very delicate mission, and one which concerns the honour, if I may use the term — "

"You may," said Hamilton, as the other paused.

" — the honour of one who is, perhaps, a dear friend of yours — Lieutenant Tibbetts."

"The devil it does!" said Hamilton in surprise. "Well, you won't be able to see Mr Tibbetts either, because he's in the bush and is unlikely to return for a week."

"Then I will stay a week," said Pinto coolly. "Perhaps you will direct me to your hotel?"

Hamilton did not like coloured people. He loved natives, he tolerated white men, but of all the types of half-breed he had reason to dislike, there was none approaching in loathsomeness to the Portuguese.

"There's a hut in the residency garden you can have," he said shortly. "Or" – as a thought struck him – "I can lend you a canoe and paddlers to take you to the Isisi River, where you will probably find Mr Tibbetts."

To his surprise, the man readily agreed to this suggestion, and it was with mingled relief and apprehension that Hamilton saw him depart, watching the grey tall hat, fascinated, until it disappeared, with its owner, round the bend of the river.

The object of Pinto's visit can be briefly stated, though in his modesty he omitted such a confession. He had come to secure £500, and he was perfectly willing to accept half. That Bones would pay rather than face an exposure he had no doubt at all. Other men had paid: a young chief clerk at Lagos had paid £300; a middle-aged Commissioner at Nigeria had paid even more before he realised what a fool he had been, and circularised a description of Mr Fernandez, *alias* Gonsalez, up and down the coast. Of this disquieting action Pinto was blissfully unaware.

The *rôle* of the outraged husband, unexpectedly appearing to the victim in the bush, away from the counsel of interfering lawyers and the devastating advice of friends, usually, in Mr Pinto's experience, had the desired effect. In Lagos, where he was known, there might have been difficulties, but even these had not arisen. Men who live in the bush carry large sums of ready money. Their belt is their banker, and Pinto did not doubt that Bones could produce from the leathern ceinture about his thin middle, sufficient to keep Pinto Fernandez and his erratic wife in comfort through many a long and pleasing siesta. As he paddled gently up the river, he did not dream of failure, and the existence of D'lama was unknown to him.

D'lama-m'popo was of the forest, and owing little but the nebulous allegiance which is given by the forest folk to the nearest paramount chief. And where loyalty is largely determined by propinquity, treason is a word which it was absurd to employ. Thus, D'lama had committed many small misdeeds, and at least one of serious importance.

D'lama owed a fisherman half a bag of salt, and the fisherman, in despair of securing a just settlement, offered D'lama the equivalent of the other half bag, together with a fat dog, a mythical cache of ivory and the freedom of the village, on condition that D'lama, who was a bachelor, took to his hut the fisherman's daughter Kobali, by her father's account a virgin, indubitably unmarried, and old by the river standard, for she had seen eighteen rainy seasons.

Now, when a woman of the river reaches the advanced age of eighteen without finding for herself a husband, a hut, and a share of the cooking, there is usually something wrong, and what was wrong with Kobali was her ability to converse with birds, a most disconcerting accomplishment, for birds know the secrets of all, since they listen in unsuspected and hidden places, and are great gossips among themselves.

There was a man in the far-away Ituri Forest who understood their cheep-twit talk, and he became a king and died honoured, and some say that on the day of his passing no bird was seen for a hundred miles.

There was another man whose career was less glorious, and there was the mad woman of Bolongo. And there was Kobali. Her father would have kept her secret, for people with supernatural powers are unpopular, and are sometimes furtively "chopped" on dark nights, but she was overseen by an elder of the village talking earnestly to three little birds that sat on a bough with their heads perked on one side, and these birds were in a state of such excitement that the elder knew that she was telling them about the wife he had left in the forest to die, because she was sick and old. And, sure enough, a week later, came Mr Commissioner Sanders with four soldiers, searching for the woman. They found all that the beasts had left, and the elder went down to the Village of Irons with a steel chain dragging from ankle to ankle.

D'lama-m'popo listened to the proposal without enthusiasm, squatting before his crazy hut and playing with the dust, from which he never raised his eyes.

"O man," he said at last, "it is true I owe you a bag-that-is-not-a-bag of salt, and when the little monkeys come back from their mysterious breeding place, I will kill many and sell them to the Government, and then I will bring you so much salt. But this woman Kobali is a witch, and who marries a witch loses his eyes. That is well known, for witches must have many eyes to see their way in the dark."

"That is foolish, D'lama," said her father – he was a mild and skinny man and incapable of violence. "For has she taken mine? She is a very fine girl…"

He proceeded to enumerate her physical attractions with a frankness which is not common in the fathers of civilisation, employing the language of superlatives which adorns the pages of a bloodstock catalogue.

"She may be this, and she may be that," said D'lama, unimpressed at the end of a long recital, "but I am a lonely man and have no wish for women."

Thereupon the father of the paragon was inspired to lie.

"The birds have told my little woman that you will take her to your hut."

Whereupon the countenance of D'lama fell. "O ko!" he said. "That means that I shall go mad! For who but a madman would take as his wife a Bird Witch? Ko ko! This is terrible to me!"

The father went back to his house by the river, and there he found Kobali sitting under a tree where the weaver birds made their home, and she was gazing upward to the excited throng above her, so intent upon all that she was hearing that until her parent had called her twice she did not heed him.

"Woman," he said, "you go to the hut of D'lama of the woods. He is a capable hunter, and he owes me salt. Now, on the last night of the moon, I will have a great dance for you."

"You make no wedding dance for me, husband of my mother," she said, "for the birds have told me that I shall marry a white man."

The jaw of the fisherman dropped. "Woman," he gasped, "now I know that you are mad! This must come in palaver before Sandi, who is near by, so that I shall not be blamed for your foolish talk."

His daughter did not quail. "The birds speak, and it is," she said simply. "Now, I tell you this, that if, in two moons, I do not marry a white man, I will go to the hut of D'lama, though he is a man of no people and is a killer of the weak. For the birds told me that he chopped an old woman for the ring she wore about her neck."

The agitated father carried the news to D'lama, who was sufficiently uncultured to show his relief.

"Who knows," he said, "that such a wonder may not happen? For this woman of yours is very cunning and understands magic, and by her cleverness she may grow a white man out of the ground."

The old fisherman blinked. "That is true, D'lama," he said, "for Kobali speaks with the birds and learns strange mysteries. This day she told me that once upon a time you killed an old woman in the bush because of the brass ring she wore upon her neck."

Being a native, D'lama did not faint, but he was silent for a very long time.

"If such things come to the ears of Sandi," he said a little huskily, "there will be a hanging palaver. Get this woman married, and I will give you more than two bags of salt."

The old man went back to his daughter and wrangled and argued with her throughout the night, without shaking her from her determination. The next morning he took his canoe and paddled three hours in the slack shore water to the juncture of the Isisi River, where a white paddle-wheel gunboat was moored while Sanders held palaver.

He sat alone in judgment, for Bones had been sent up the Isisi River to arrest a certain petty chief who had sanctioned witchcraft in his territory. Under the striped awning on the after-deck of the *Zaire* Sanders listened to complaints, tried matrimonial suits, offered advice and admonition briefly and, at times, a little brutally. To him came the fisherman with his story of woe. Sanders listened without interruption until, in the way of litigants, the old man began his recital over again.

"Go back to your daughter, fisherman," said Sanders, "and tell her that white men do not marry black women – in my territory. And if she be, as you say, a witch, then there is punishment for that, as all the lands and people know."

"Lord," said the fisherman, "she speaks with the birds, and they tell her she will come to no harm."

"She has not spoken with the right bird," said Sanders grimly, and dismissed him.

It was the end of the palaver, and he rose a little stiffly, and walked forward, leaning over the rail and watching incuriously the broad river flowing to the sea. As he looked, there came into his zone of vision a long canoe, which he recognised, by its shape and the rhythmical action of the paddlers, as from headquarters. He lifted a pair of binoculars and scanned the oncoming craft, expecting to find Hamilton in the little leaf-roofed cabin at the stern.

"Jumping Moses!" said Sanders, and, putting down the glasses, he waited until the canoe drew alongside and Mr Pinto Fernandez, complete in grey top hat and somewhat soiled white spats, stepped on board.

"Mr Tibbetts, I presume?" said Pinto sternly.

Sanders smiled. "No, I am not Mr Tibbetts," he said. "I am the Commissioner in these parts. What can I do for you, my man?"

"I wish to see Mr Tibbetts on a matter of delicacy and honour," said Pinto glibly, and Sanders' eyes narrowed.

"Take off your hat," he said curtly; "you needn't fear sunstroke. You are a coloured man, I see."

"I am a Portuguese subject," said Pinto with dignity, but obeyed.

Sanders looked at him for a very long time, "Now, will you please tell me the object of your visit?" he said softly.

"It is a matter for Mr Tibbetts' ears alone."

"It is nothing to do, by any chance, with a correspondence in which Mr Tibbetts has been engaged?" asked Sanders, and did not fail to observe the start of surprise. "Because there was a gentleman, if I remember rightly, in Nigeria, who had an indiscreet correspondence with a lady in Funchal, and was induced to part with a considerable sum of money," said Sanders. "That fact came to me through official correspondence. What is your name?"

"Gonsalez," said Pinto,

Sanders rubbed his chin thoughtfully. "That isn't the name – but I seem to remember your face," he said. "I have seen a photograph somewhere – oh yes, your name is Pinto Fernandez, and you are wanted by the Nigerian police for embezzlement. Curiously enough" – he was speaking as though to himself – "I never connected you with the ingenious blackmailer, and I don't suppose anybody else has."

"I want to say, Mr Sanders," said Pinto loudly, and slightly flustered, "that your Tibbetts has been corresponding with my foolish wife – "

Sanders stopped him with a gesture. "According to the police report I have had from Nigeria, that was the basis of your argument with another gentleman."

He beckoned the watchful Abiboo. "Put this man in irons," he said.

Pinto Fernandez had been in many tight corners, and he was a man of considerable initiative. Before the sergeant's hand fell on his arm, he jumped to the taffrail and leapt the four or five feet which separated the *Zaire* from the bank. Before the Houssa could raise his rifle, he had plunged into the bush, leaving behind, as a souvenir of his presence, a grey topper and the nearly gold-headed walking-stick, which he carried as part of the insignia of his respectability.

He heard the sound of a shot and the whine and patter of a bullet as it flicked through the leaves of the trees, and sprinted along the narrow native track into the forest. He was no stranger to the wild lands, and had the bush instinct which led him unerringly to the broader native road that ran parallel with the river bank. In the early hours of the morning he came to a little clearing, and D'lama-m'popo, coming out of his hut, stood stock still at the startling apparition.

"Oh master, I see you," said D'lama respectfully.

Pinto, who knew most of the dialects of the rivers, answered readily.

"Give me food, man," he said. "I am going on a long journey for Sandi. Also I want sleep, for I have walked through the forest, battling with wild beasts, all this night. And if any ask you about me you shall be silent, for it is Sandi's desire that no man should know that I am hereabouts."

D'lama prepared a meal, brought water from the forest spring, and left his guest to sleep. That evening, Pinto was wakened by the entry of his host.

"Man, Sandi wants you," said D'lama, "for this is the talk amongst all the villagers, that a certain one was taken prisoner by Sandi and escaped, and the master has sent word that you must be taken."

"That is fool's talk," said Pinto. "You see I am a white man, wearing trousers."

D'lama surveyed him critically. "That is true, for you are not quite black," he said. "Now, if you are a white man, then I have a wonderful thought in my head. For hereabouts lives a witch who talks with birds, and the birds told her that she should marry a white man, and after that the land should prosper."

"I am already married," said Pinto hastily.

"Who is not?" asked the crude D'lama. "Yet you shall marry her, and I will be silent. And no people live in this forest who talk – except the birds. If you say no; then I will take you to Sandi, and there is an end. But if you say you will marry, then I will bring this girl to you."

"Bring the woman," said Pinto after a moment's thought; but whatever plans he had formed were purposeless.

"First I will tie you by the hands and feet," said D'lama calmly, "lest when I am gone, an evil spirit comes into your heart and you run away."

And Pinto, protesting, allowed himself to be trussed, for D'lama-m'popo was a man of inches and terribly strong.

The woman who talked with birds was in her old place beneath the nests of the weaver birds when D'lama arrived.

"You are D'lama, the killer of old women," she said, not looking round, "and a bird has told me that you have found a white man."

"That is true, Kobali," said D'lama, in a sweat, "and as to the old woman, a tree fell upon her –"

Kobali rose silently and led the way into the forest, D'lama following. After a while they came to the hut where Pinto lay, in some pain, and together they brought him out into the light of the moon, and the girl examined him critically whilst the bonds were being removed.

"He is a white that is not black, and a black that is not white," she said. "I think this man will do for me, for he seems very pretty."

Pinto's hand rose mechanically to twirl his sparse moustache.

★ ★ ★

"I can't really understand what happened to that fellow," said Sanders. "He must have got in the track of a leopard."

"Or the leopard must have got on his," suggested Hamilton. "By the way, what did he want with Bones?"

But Sanders shook his head. He was a model of discretion, and Bones, in his many journeys up and down the river, never guessed that from behind the bush that fringed the river near the Isisi, dwelt one who, in happier circumstances, had described himself as Dom Gonsalez, and who possessed a very charming wife in the town of Funchal — or did possess her until she got tired of waiting, and contracted a morganatic marriage with the second officer of a banana boat out of Cadiz.

THE LAKE OF THE DEVIL

M'suru, an Akasava chief of some importance, was hunting one day on the wrong side of the Ochori frontier when there appeared, at a most unpropitious moment, a man called Mabidini, who was something that was neither ranger nor hunter, yet was a little of each, for he watched the frontiers for his lord Bosambo, and poached skins secretly in the Akasava country.

He was a young man, and, by the standards which are set by the women of the Upper River, handsome; and these qualities made his subsequent offence the more unforgivable, for M'suru was middle-aged and fat and past the attractive period of life, so that only the women he bought were his, and nobody did anything for love of him. Mabidini, on the contrary, crooked his finger, and where was the marriage bond?

Inauspicious the moment, for M'suru was skinning a great water buck, and his four huntsmen had the skin stretched for salting.

"O ko!" said Mabidini. "This is bad news for Boambo my chief! No man hunts in this wood but he."

M'sura wiped the sweat out of his eyes with the back of the hand that held the skinning knife.

"Who sees, knows," he said significantly. "You shall have the fore-part of this meat for your pot."

But Mabidini desired neither flesh nor skin, and the word went to Bosambo, and eventually to Mr Commissioner Sanders, and M'suru paid ten bags of salt by way of fine. Worse than this, he became the

171

mock of such as Mabidini, a man without a village, who dwelt in a hut in the very heart of the wood and had no people.

One night six strange warriors slipped into the forest, and, taking Mabidini from his hut, they flogged him with skin whips, and burnt his toes so that he hobbled for months. That his assailants were Akasava he did not doubt; he would sooner have believed that he was dead than that M'suru did not instigate the outrage.

One day Bosambo sent for him. "Mabidini, I have spoken with Sandi, who is my own brother, and he says there can be no palaver over this matter of your beating, because none knows, and M'suru, who knows, lies," he said. "They say of M'suru that he has a magic spear and therefore is very powerful. Also he has a new wife whom he bought for ten thousand brass rods. You are a lonely man, and it seems that, if men attack you in the night, such a spear would save you from having your toes burnt. For your wife would alarm you, and the spear would be under your bed."

"Lord, I have no wife," said Mabidini, who was no more dense than any man of the Ochori.

"Nor spear," said Bosambo.

So Mabidini took a canoe and drifted down to within a mile or two of the village where his enemy dwelt, and one day he saw, walking in the forest, a girl who cried and rubbed the weals on her shoulders. He knew her to be M'suru's wife and spoke to her. At first she was frightened...

Night fell suddenly on the village of Kolobafa and was welcomed by the third wife of M'suru, for there was a deficiency in her household equipment which her lord, with his fox-eyes, would have seen instantly. As it was, he came home too tired and hungry to be suspicious, and, having had his fill sitting solitary before the little fire that smouldered in front of the hut, he nodded and dozed until the chill of the night sent him in a daze of sleep to find his skin bed. The third (and newest) wife, whose name was Kimi, sat aloof, watching in an agony of apprehension, and when he had gone into the hut clasped her bare sides with such force that she ached.

But no bull-roar of fury proclaimed the discovery of his loss, and, creeping to the side of the hut, she listened, heard his snores and crept back.

She enjoyed a hut of her own, and the jealous elder wife, brooding in the dark doorway of the hut she shared with the ousted second, saw Kimi steal away through the village street, and called shrilly to her companion, for, if she hated the second wife, she hated Kimi worst, and in such a crisis lesser enemies have the appearance of friends.

"Kimi has gone to the river to see her lover. Let us wake M'suru and tell him."

The second wife thrust her blunt head over the stout shoulder that filled the doorway, and peered after the vanishing girl.

"M'suru sends his spears at night to the N'gombi man, who sharpens them on a stone. If we wake M'suru with a foolish story he will beat us."

"She carried no spears," said the first wife, contemptuously. "You are afraid." Suddenly a thought struck her. "If she carries any spear, it will be the Spear of the Ghost!"

There was a shocked "huh!" from the second wife, for the Spear of the Ghost had come to M'suru from his father, and from his father's father, and from countless generations of fathers. It was a short killing spear, endowed with magical qualities. By its potency M'suru could perform miracles. The broad blade dipped into the river brought back the fish which, for some reason, had deserted the known spearing places; carried into the forest, its magic peopled the woods with prey; but its greatest property was this: if a man were lost in the deep forest he had but to balance the spear on his fingertip and the blade pointed unerringly to safety.

It had many other qualities, curious and awe-inspiring. Thus, all other spears leapt toward the king spear, and could not be drawn away except by great force.

Even the elder wife of M'suru could not screw her courage into waking her lord. It was not until the chief of Kolobafa came out blinking into the daylight and bellowed for his wife, that the loss was discovered. For lost indeed was the magic spear!

Mr Commissioner Sanders was holding a palaver by the Crocodile's Pool over a matter of belated taxation, and M'suru, in full panoply, attended to lay before him his great complaint.

"Lord," he said, "a terrible misfortune has come upon me and my people. My wife had a lover, whose name is Mabidini, a man of the Ochori tribe and well known to you because he swore falsely against me. Because this woman loved him, she went to him when I slept, taking the Spear of the Ghost, which, as your lordship knows, is the most holy spear in the world, and there is none other like it. Therefore I come to you for leave to carry my spears into the Ochori country."

"O ko," said Sanders sardonically, "what manner of man are you that you set yourself up to punish? For it seems that I am nothing in this land, and M'suru, a little chief of the Akasava, can take my place. As for your spear, it is made of a certain iron which I know well."

He called for his orderly, gave an order in Arabic, and Abiboo went away, to return with a small steel magnet.

"Look well at this, M'suru; for if your spear is magic, so then is this little thing that is shaped like the bend of the lost river that runs to Bura-Ladi."

Sanders took the spear from the chief's hand and put the magnet against it.

"Now pull your spear," he said, and it required a jerk to break the weapon from the magnet's influence.

"There shall be no killing and no carrying of spears, M'suru," he said. "It seems to me that already you know the Ochori country so well that your young warriors can find their paths in the dark! When I go back to my fine house by the sea I will have another spear made for you, and it will be called the Spear of Sanders, and you shall hold it for me and my king. As to the woman, if she has a lover, you may put her away according to the law. I shall return when the moon is new, and you shall bring the matter before me. The palaver is finished."

M'suru, in no way satisfied, went back to his village and called together the elder men and such friends as he had – which were few, for he was a notoriously severe man and in no sense popular.

"In two days from now Sandi will go back to his fine house by the river, and his spies will go with him; for it is well known that in the days which follow the palavers the spies do not watch, for all people fear Sandi. Therefore, send your young spearmen to me in the first hour of the night, and I will lead you to the hut of Mabidini, and we will take the spear which belongs to me, and such goats and women as we may find."

The way to the hut was a long one, for the Ochori territory throws into the Akasava a deep, knife-shaped peninsula, and a true peninsula in the sense that it is bordered by a river which has no appearance except in the wet season. And this has to be avoided. There is water enough at all times, but the rank grass grows quickly, and here all manner of strange, aqueous beasts have their dwellings. This river, F'giri, runs to that deep, still lake which is called Kafa-guri — literally, "the hole in the world."

On the fourth day M'suru fetched up at the deserted hut of his enemy, and learnt by inquiry from a wandering bushman that Mabidini had gone eastward to the silent lake.

"This man is not afraid, because he has my spear, which is very powerful against ghosts," said M'suru when he heard the news and followed, for the secret river was in flood. But his warriors did not know his objective.

★   ★   ★

"I don't like the look of Bones," said Hamilton, glowering under the rim of his topee at the figure which was approaching the residency with long strides.

Sanders knocked the ash from his cheroot and smiled.

"The impression I have is that you never have been enamoured of Bones' personal appearance," he said.

"I'm not referring to his general homeliness," said Hamilton. "My concentrated antipathy is directed to the particular Bones who is at present visible to the naked eye. I dislike Bones when he struts," he growled, "because when he struts he is pleased with himself, and when Bones is pleased with himself it is time for all modest men to take cover. Good morning, Bones. Why the smirk?"

Bones saluted jerkily. He had a habit of bringing up his hand and allowing it to quiver – no other word describes the motion – within half an inch of the helmet.

"I wish to heaven you'd learn to salute properly," snapped Hamilton. "I'd give you two hours' saluting drill for two pins!"

"But, dear old officer, this is the very latest," said Bones calmly, and repeated the action. "I saw a stunning old sergeant of the Guards do it. What is good enough for the jolly old Grenadiers is good enough for poor old Bones. I think you said 'smirk'?"

He put his hand up to his ear as though he was anxious not to lose a word.

"Stand to attention, you insubordinate hound," said Hamilton. "And if you're deaf you'd better report and see a – a – "

"Oculist is the word you want, dear old Ham – oculist, from the word 'hark,' sometimes pronounced 'harkulist.' "

"You seem pleased with yourself, Bones," interposed Sanders hastily.

"Not so much pleased, dear old excellency," said Bones, "as what you might describe as grateified."

"You mean gratified," said Hamilton.

"Great, grateful, grateified," retorted Bones reproachfully. "Dear old thing, you're all wrong this morning. What's the matter with you? Jolly old liver out of condition?"

He pulled up a chair, sat down, and, resting his chin on his palms, glared across to him.

"Have you ever thought, dear old officer," he asked in the hollow voice he invariably assumed when he became profound, "that here we are, living in this strange and almost wild country! We know this place, we know the river – it is water; we know the land – it is land; we know the dinky old flora and the jolly old fauna, and yet we are perhaps ignorant of the very longitude and latitude of, so to speak, our jolly old native home!"

He stopped, inserted his monocle, and glared triumphantly at the dazed Hamilton.

"What the devil are you talking about?"

"Has it occurred to you, dear old thing, that we should not be here if it were not for the brave and intrepid souls who, so to speak, have blazed a path through the jolly old wilderness?"

Hamilton looked at Sanders in alarm. "Have you any quinine, sir?" he asked.

"No, no, dear old medical one, I am not suffering from fever; I am, in fact, *non compos mentis*, to employ a Latin phrase."

"That is what I'm suggesting," said Hamilton.

"Has it ever occurred to you — ?" Bones went on, but Hamilton stopped him.

"The thing that is occurring to me at the moment is that you've been drinking, Bones."

"Me, sir?" said the indignant Bones. "That's an actionable statement, dear old officer. As a scientist, I — "

"Oh, you're a scientist, are you? Knew there was something queer about you. What branch of science is suffering from your malignant association?"

Bones smiled tolerantly. "I was merely pointing out, dear old member of the jolly old public, that if it hadn't been for our explorers — Livingstone, Stanley — in fact, dear old thing, I've been elected a Member of the Royal Geographical Society."

He drew back in his chair to watch the effect.

"That is fine, Bones," said Sanders. "I congratulate you. How did you become a member?"

"By paying a guinea or two," said the scornful Hamilton. "Anybody can become a member if he pays his subscription."

"You're wrong, my boy," said Bones. "I wrote a dinky little article on the etymological peculiarities of native tribes; in other words, the difference between one set of native johnnies and another set of native johnnies."

"Good Lord!" gasped Hamilton. "Did you call it 'etymological'?"

"Naturally," said Bones calmly. "There is no other word."

Captain Hamilton's face was a study. "Etymology," he said gently, "is that branch of grammar which deals with the derivation of words, you poor fish! The word you were labouring after was 'ethnology.' Did you call it etymology?"

"I did," said Bones calmly, "and the dear old johnnies quite understood what I meant. After all, you don't have to spell to discover the source of the Nile, dear old thing. You haven't to be a jolly old whale on grammar to trace the source of the Congo. Many of us explorers – "

"Shut up about 'us'," said Hamilton. "And, talking of exploring, I shall want you to explore – "

"Don't tell me that that pay sheet is wrong again, dear old officer," said Bones sternly. "If it is, it is your doing." He pointed an accusing finger at his superior. "I've been through it six times, and I made the same result every time. If it is wrong, there is foul play somewhere – jolly foul!"

That the conversation should not drift to the horrid subject of work, he produced a letter he had received that morning. It was from a Fellow of the Society, and a very learned fellow indeed.

"DEAR MR TIBBETTS," the letter ran, "I was very interested in your interesting paper on the ethnological peculiarities of the Bantu tribes, which I had the pleasure of revising for publication – "

"I knew somebody corrected the spelling," murmured Hamilton.

"I wonder if you will ever have an opportunity of giving us more information on the subject of the lakes in your country, some of which, I believe, have never been explored. Particularly am I anxious to know more on the subject of one lake, Bura-Ladi, about which many stories are in existence."

Sanders looked up quickly. There were in his territory many unexplored patches, and Bura-Ladi was one of these. This small, still lake lay in a depression that was popularly supposed to be bottomless. No fish were found therein. Fishermen avoided it; even the beasts in the forest never came down to drink at its margin, and the earth around it was bare for a quarter of a mile.

Sanders had seen the place twice: a lonely, sinister spot.

"There will be a chance for you, Bones, and in the very near future," said Sanders. "You have never seen the lake?"

"I haven't, for the matter of that," said Hamilton, and Bones uttered an impatient tut-tut.

"Dear old Ham," he said gently, "the jolly old Commissioner is discussing this matter with *me*, dear old thing. Don't be peeved; I can quite understand it, old Ham, but this is a matter of science."

"So was your last essay," said Hamilton significantly, and Bones coughed.

"That, old sir, was pure fantasy, old officer. A little *jeu d'esprit* in the style of the late Lewis Carrots – Alice's Wonderful Land. Perhaps you haven't read the book, dear old soldier. If you haven't you ought to get it straight away; it is horribly amusing."

"I think you told the misguided and gullible editor of the *Guildford Times* that you had discovered a new kind of okapi with two tails," said Hamilton remorselessly. "And – correct me if I'm wrong – you said that in the Forest of Dreams you had come upon a new monkey family that wore clothes. As the nearest Italian organ-grinder is some three thousand miles away, I take leave to describe you as an ingenious prevaricator. Now, the point is, Bones, what novelty are you going to find in Bura-Ladi?"

"It is queer," Sanders broke in thoughtfully. "Do you know the temperature of the lake is about twelve degrees higher than the temperature of the river? In the rainy season, when one can get a cold spell, I've seen the lake steaming. No native will live within twenty miles of the place. They say there is neither fish nor crocodile in its waters. I've been making up my mind for eight years to make a very thorough exploration. And now, Bones," he said with a smile, "you've taken the job out of my hands."

179

Hamilton sniffed. "And he'll find more in ten minutes than Darwin would have discovered in twenty years. After all, a little imagination is a great help."

Bones reached out and gripped the unwilling hand of his senior.

"Thank you, dear old Ham," he said gratefully. "That's just what I've got. You've been a jolly long time finding out my good points, but better late than never, dear old sir and officer, better late than never!"

A month later, when Sanders went up river on his taxation palaver, he dropped Lieutenant Tibbetts at the point where the river comes nearest to the lake.

"And, Bones!"

Hamilton leant over the side of the *Zaire* as the canoe was pulling away.

"No funny stories, Bones! No discovery of prehistoric animals frisking in the depths of the lake. Science, Bones – pure science!"

Bones smiled pityingly. He found it easier to smile pityingly than to think of an appropriate retort.

The day he reached the edge of the lake there came a man and woman overland.

"Here we will stay, Kimi, until M'suru returns, for he will not follow us here owing to ghosts."

Bones knew nothing of this.

★ ★ ★

There came a letter to headquarters by messenger.

"Dear sir dear sir and Exerlency" (wrote Bones) "I have the hounour to report that I reached I reached Lake Boorar-Ladi at eleven at eleven oclock this morning morning. I have made a Camp on the North side. Dear sir the most extreordinry thing has happened the most extery extro extronary thing has happend. There has been a vulcanic eruption! At nine oclock tonight there was a tarrific noise in the lake the lake! It came from the derection of the lake the lake. On preceding to the

spot I found the waters in a state of great upheval upheeval and
by the light of the moon I saw that an ireland had appeared in
the middle of the lake. The ireland was smoking steamishly. It
was nearly a hundread yards in lenth length. Owing to absence
of nessessary transport (canoe raft etc.) I was unable to make
close investeragation. This morning another tarrific explosion
occured and the ireland disappeared."

"I hope he means 'island,' " said Sanders, "but we have no volcanic
patches in this territory. Now, if we were near Kilamansaro – "

"I imagine Bones is preparing his report for his unfortunate
college," said Hamilton drily.

But in the night Sanders was wakened by the sergeant of the guard.

"Lord, the beater of the *lokali* says that there is bad trouble by the
hot lake, and that Tibbetti has fought M'suru and has been taken
prisoner."

A few minutes later Sanders knocked at the door of Hamilton's
bedroom.

"The *Zaire* leaves at daybreak," he said.

★ ★ ★

A spy came to M'suru with news of the fugitives.

"They have made a hut near the Lake of Devils," he said. "Also,
M'suru, there have been terrible happenings, for land came up from
the water and then went down again."

M'suru had some difficulty in persuading his followers to continue
with him, but at last the terror he could inspire overcame their fear of
the unknown and they went on, and as the sun was setting their
fearful eyes rested on the sombre scene.

In a vast desert of yellow earth the lake lay blood-red in the dying
light of the sun. lt was shaped like an egg, and on the narrower end a
misty blue haze rested.

"O ko, this is bad!" said M'suru in dismay, and pointed.

On the farther shore his sharp eyes had seen the moored canoe, and on the slope above the tiny green tent that marked the tent of Lieutenant Tibbetts.

"Sandi!" said one of M'suru's men, and the chief snarled round at him.

"You are a fool," he said, "for Sandi is on his big ship. Therefore this must be a trader. Show me where Kimi and the man live."

The spy pointed to a far green belt, and M'suru grunted his satisfaction.

In the hour before the dawn he reached the hut, and not all the magic of the Ghost Spear availed Mabidini. Him they crucified to a tree. Kimi died earlier and more mercifully. Bones, in the frenzy of exploration, heard the shrieks and went, revolver in hand, to discover the cause.

"I see you, Mabidini!"

M'suru was frothing at the mouth as he howled his hate at the dying man. He heard a shout behind him and turned, his spear poised.

Twice Bones fired and twice missed. The second shot struck the tortured Mabidini and passed him out of the world. Then, in a frenzy of fear, one of M'suru's men threw a spear. The point caught the bough of a bush, but the ironwood handle, spinning round, struck Bones in the throat, and he stumbled, gasping.

For a second M'suru hesitated, his spear raised, and then the knowledge that the white man would not be alone decided him. He flew down the slope toward the lake, his followers behind him. Far away to the left he saw the red tarboshes of two Houssas. They were at such a distance that he could safely make for the camp where the canoe was moored.

He saw the soldiers running, heard the wrathful yell of Bones racing behind, and made his decision. He was in the canoe, hacking with his razor-sharp hunting spear at the native rope that bound it.

"Shoot!" roared Bones.

The Houssas dropped to their knees, and two bullets struck the water left and right of the racing canoe.

M'suru was steering for the opposite bank, and Bones knew enough of native marksmanship to hope that anything but a chance bullet would catch the flying murderer.

"Cease fire," he ordered as the breathless soldiery came up to him. M'suru would keep.

"Go back to a little hut by the trees and bury a woman; also take down Mabidini of the Ochori, who is fastened by a spear to a tree," he said, and, when the men's backs were turned, watched the canoe.

It had reached the centre of the lake, and the paddles were moving more leisurely.

"You nasty fellow," said Bones, and said no more, staring openmouthed at what he saw.

The surface of the lake had become strangely agitated. Great waves were sweeping outward toward the shores, and in the middle there appeared a dark mass, which must have been at least two hundred feet in length.

The men in the canoe were at the western end of the amazing upheaval, and M'suru, seeing the thing, changed his course.

He saw more than Bones, for suddenly the canoe turned and came back toward the camp, the paddlers working frantically.

And then there came up from the depths of the lake a great spade-shaped head. It rose higher and higher at the end of a neck that seemed thin in comparison. Towering over the canoe, the head darted down with incredible swiftness. There was a huge splash. Bones, frozen with horror, saw the head moving about in the water, as the bill of a duck moves when feeding. Another second, and the island had disappeared, and only two fragments of the canoe broke the smooth expanse of water.

★ ★ ★

"I *knew* that you'd see an ichthyosaurus," said Hamilton. "Bones, you're incorrigible! You had two fellows there who could have corroborated your yarn, and what did you do with 'em? Sent them away! Oh, Bones, Bones!"

Lieutenant Tibbetts groaned in the agony of his soul.

"My dear old officer... I saw it! A hundred yards long, old officer... I *wasn't* dreaming." He was almost in tears.

The *Zaire* had pushed her way through the weed-grown river, and lay under the sloping bank of the lake. Sanders had listened in silence to the narrative of his subordinate.

"Bones, I believe you," he said, to Hamilton's amazement.

"You believe it, sir?"

Sanders nodded. "Such things have been seen in the volcanic areas in East Africa...it is possible."

He had intended returning immediately he had discovered that the garbled story of Bones' capture was untrue — to what watchful tribesman he owed the warning he never discovered. But now he decided to wait, and again, to Hamilton's surprise, had the *Zaire* taken back to the Little River.

"But surely, sir — " began Hamilton.

"You never know," said Sanders.

He spent the night with Hamilton, filling a small iron water-tank with a variety of explosives, and the Captain of Houssas warmed to his task. In the early morning Hamilton fixed a time fuse, and the tank, balanced on the steamer's foredeck, was ready to drop as the *Zaire* moved slowly to midstream.

"Take the starboard gun, Bones," said Sanders, and Bones crouched at the Hotchkiss, his finger on the brass trigger.

"I don't know whether I'm dreaming," said Hamilton, "but I certainly feel that Bones is going to owe us an apology after this!"

Sanders swung the *Zaire* to midstream, and, jamming over the telegraph to full speed, gave a signal to the Houssas in the bow. The tank dropped with a splash as the *Zaire* swung round and headed for the river, her stern wheel revolving furiously. They reached the weed-grown river mouth and slowed.

"That will do," said Sanders, watch in hand, and stopped the engines.

"Bones!" whispered his superior. "You've fooled the Commissioner!"

At that moment there was a quivering thud of sound – a white geyser of water leapt up in the centre of the lake, and – that was all.

"Nothing!" said Hamilton.

The word was hardly out of his mouth when the waters of the lake began to rock and toss, and out of the depths arose that horrible spade-shaped head. Higher and higher the neck emerged.

"Bang!"

The Hotchkiss spat viciously, and somewhere near the fearful head a blue-black ball of smoke came into being. When it had gone there was no head – nothing but the boiling, bubbling waters and the flash of a great, dead-white surface like the belly of a fish.

"I wouldn't write about this if I were you, Bones," said Sanders later.

"Dear old sir," confessed Bones, "my jolly old hand is too shaky to write – I'm stickin' to the dinkey little monkeys with pants."

EDGAR WALLACE

BIG FOOT

Footprints and a dead woman bring together Superintendent Minton and the amateur sleuth Mr Cardew. Who is the man in the shrubbery? Who is the singer of the haunting Moorish tune? Why is Hannah Shaw so determined to go to Pawsy, 'a dog lonely place' she had previously detested? Death lurks in the dark and someone must solve the mystery before BIG FOOT strikes again, in a yet more fiendish manner.

BONES IN LONDON

The new Managing Director of Schemes Ltd has an elegant London office and a theatrically dressed assistant − however Bones, as he is better known, is bored. Luckily there is a slump in the shipping market and it is not long before Joe and Fred Pole pay Bones a visit. They are totally unprepared for Bones' unnerving style of doing business, unprepared for his unique style of innocent and endearing mischief.

Edgar Wallace

The Daffodil Mystery

When Mr Thomas Lyne, poet, poseur and owner of Lyne's Emporium insults a cashier, Odette Rider, she resigns. Having summoned detective Jack Tarling to investigate another employee, Mr Milburgh, Lyne now changes his plans. Tarling and his Chinese companion refuse to become involved. They pay a visit to Odette's flat. In the hall Tarling meets Sam, convicted felon and protégé of Lyne. Next morning Tarling discovers a body. The hands are crossed on the breast, adorned with a handful of daffodils.

The Joker

While the millionaire Stratford Harlow is in Princetown, not only does he meet with his lawyer Mr Ellenbury but he gets his first glimpse of the beautiful Aileen Rivers, niece of the actor and convicted felon Arthur Ingle. When Aileen is involved in a car accident on the Thames Embankment, the driver is James Carlton of Scotland Yard. Later that evening Carlton gets a call. It is Aileen. She needs help.

EDGAR WALLACE

THE SQUARE EMERALD

'Suicide on the left,' says Chief Inspector Coldwell pleasantly, as he and Leslie Maughan stride along the Thames Embankment during a brutally cold night. A gaunt figure is sprawled across the parapet. But Coldwell soon discovers that Peter Dawlish, fresh out of prison for forgery, is not considering suicide but murder. Coldwell suspects Druze as the intended victim. Maughan disagrees. If Druze dies, she says, 'It will be because he does not love children!'

THE THREE OAK MYSTERY

While brothers Lexington and Socrates Smith, authority on fingerprints and blood stains, are guests of Peter Mandle and his stepdaughter, they observe a light flashing from the direction of Mr Jethroe's house. COME THREE OAKS, it spells in Morse. A ghostly figure is seen hurrying across the moonlit lawn. Early next morning the brothers take a stroll, and there, tied to an oak branch, is a body – a purple mark where the bullet struck.

OTHER TITLES BY EDGAR WALLACE AVAILABLE DIRECT
FROM HOUSE OF STRATUS

Quantity	£	$(US)	$(CAN)	€
THE ADMIRABLE CARFEW	6.99	11.50	15.99	11.50
THE ANGEL OF TERROR	6.99	11.50	15.99	11.50
THE AVENGER	6.99	11.50	15.99	11.50
BARBARA ON HER OWN	6.99	11.50	15.99	11.50
BIG FOOT	6.99	11.50	15.99	11.50
THE BLACK ABBOT	6.99	11.50	15.99	11.50
BONES	6.99	11.50	15.99	11.50
BONES IN LONDON	6.99	11.50	15.99	11.50
THE CLUE OF THE NEW PIN	6.99	11.50	15.99	11.50
THE CLUE OF THE SILVER KEY	6.99	11.50	15.99	11.50
THE CLUE OF THE TWISTED CANDLE	6.99	11.50	15.99	11.50
THE COAT OF ARMS	6.99	11.50	15.99	11.50
THE COUNCIL OF JUSTICE	6.99	11.50	15.99	11.50
THE CRIMSON CIRCLE	6.99	11.50	15.99	11.50
THE DAFFODIL MYSTERY	6.99	11.50	15.99	11.50
THE DARK EYES OF LONDON	6.99	11.50	15.99	11.50
THE DAUGHTERS OF THE NIGHT	6.99	11.50	15.99	11.50
A DEBT DISCHARGED	6.99	11.50	15.99	11.50
THE DEVIL MAN	6.99	11.50	15.99	11.50
THE DOOR WITH SEVEN LOCKS	6.99	11.50	15.99	11.50
THE DUKE IN THE SUBURBS	6.99	11.50	15.99	11.50
THE FACE IN THE NIGHT	6.99	11.50	15.99	11.50
THE FEATHERED SERPENT	6.99	11.50	15.99	11.50
THE FLYING SQUAD	6.99	11.50	15.99	11.50
THE FORGER	6.99	11.50	15.99	11.50
THE FOUR JUST MEN	6.99	11.50	15.99	11.50
FOUR SQUARE JANE	6.99	11.50	15.99	11.50
THE FOURTH PLAGUE	6.99	11.50	15.99	11.50

ALL HOUSE OF STRATUS BOOKS ARE AVAILABLE FROM GOOD BOOKSHOPS
OR DIRECT FROM THE PUBLISHER:

Internet: www.houseofstratus.com including author interviews, reviews, features.

Email: sales@houseofstratus.com please quote author, title and credit card details.

OTHER TITLES BY EDGAR WALLACE AVAILABLE DIRECT
FROM HOUSE OF STRATUS

Quantity	£	$(US)	$(CAN)	€
THE FRIGHTENED LADY	6.99	11.50	15.99	11.50
GOOD EVANS	6.99	11.50	15.99	11.50
THE HAND OF POWER	6.99	11.50	15.99	11.50
THE IRON GRIP	6.99	11.50	15.99	11.50
THE JOKER	6.99	11.50	15.99	11.50
THE JUST MEN OF CORDOVA	6.99	11.50	15.99	11.50
THE KEEPERS OF THE KING'S PEACE	6.99	11.50	15.99	11.50
THE LAW OF THE FOUR JUST MEN	6.99	11.50	15.99	11.50
THE LONE HOUSE MYSTERY	6.99	11.50	15.99	11.50
THE MAN WHO BOUGHT LONDON	6.99	11.50	15.99	11.50
THE MAN WHO KNEW	6.99	11.50	15.99	11.50
THE MAN WHO WAS NOBODY	6.99	11.50	15.99	11.50
THE MIND OF MR J G REEDER	6.99	11.50	15.99	11.50
MORE EDUCATED EVANS	6.99	11.50	15.99	11.50
MR J G REEDER RETURNS	6.99	11.50	15.99	11.50
MR JUSTICE MAXWELL	6.99	11.50	15.99	11.50
RED ACES	6.99	11.50	15.99	11.50
ROOM 13	6.99	11.50	15.99	11.50
SANDERS	6.99	11.50	15.99	11.50
SANDERS OF THE RIVER	6.99	11.50	15.99	11.50
THE SINISTER MAN	6.99	11.50	15.99	11.50
THE SQUARE EMERALD	6.99	11.50	15.99	11.50
THE THREE JUST MEN	6.99	11.50	15.99	11.50
THE THREE OAK MYSTERY	6.99	11.50	15.99	11.50
THE TRAITOR'S GATE	6.99	11.50	15.99	11.50
WHEN THE GANGS CAME TO LONDON	6.99	11.50	15.99	11.50
WHEN THE WORLD STOPPED	6.99	11.50	15.99	11.50

Hotline: UK ONLY: 0800 169 1780, please quote author, title and credit card details.
INTERNATIONAL: +44 (0) 20 7494 6400, please quote author, title and
credit card details.

Send to: **House of Stratus Sales Department**
24c Old Burlington Street
London
W1X 1RL
UK

Please allow for postage costs charged per order plus an amount per book as set out in the tables below:

	£(Sterling)	$(US)	$(CAN)	€(Euros)
Cost per order				
UK	2.00	3.00	4.50	3.30
Europe	3.00	4.50	6.75	5.00
North America	3.00	4.50	6.75	5.00
Rest of World	3.00	4.50	6.75	5.00
Additional cost per book				
UK	0.50	0.75	1.15	0.85
Europe	1.00	1.50	2.30	1.70
North America	2.00	3.00	4.60	3.40
Rest of World	2.50	3.75	5.75	4.25

PLEASE SEND CHEQUE, POSTAL ORDER (STERLING ONLY), EUROCHEQUE, OR INTERNATIONAL MONEY ORDER (PLEASE CIRCLE METHOD OF PAYMENT YOU WISH TO USE)
MAKE PAYABLE TO: STRATUS HOLDINGS plc

Cost of book(s): ———————— Example: 3 x books at £6.99 each: £20.97
Cost of order: ———————— Example: £2.00 (Delivery to UK address)
Additional cost per book: ———————— Example: 3 x £0.50: £1.50
Order total including postage: ———————— Example: £24.47

Please tick currency you wish to use and add total amount of order:

☐ £ (Sterling) ☐ $ (US) ☐ $ (CAN) ☐ € (EUROS)

VISA, MASTERCARD, SWITCH, AMEX, SOLO, JCB:

☐ ☐ ☐ ☐ ☐ ☐ ☐ ☐ ☐ ☐ ☐ ☐ ☐ ☐ ☐ ☐ ☐ ☐ ☐

Issue number (Switch only):

☐ ☐ ☐

Start Date: **Expiry Date:**

☐ ☐ / ☐ ☐   ☐ ☐ / ☐ ☐

Signature: ————————————————

NAME: ————————————————————————

ADDRESS: ——————————————————————

——————————————————————————

POSTCODE: ——————————

Please allow 28 days for delivery.

Prices subject to change without notice.
Please tick box if you do not wish to receive any additional information. ☐

House of Stratus publishes many other titles in this genre; please check our website (**www.houseofstratus.com**) for more details.